"Nostalgia isn't part of his equation. [Indiana is] the author of seven novels, and a prolific essayist and critic; he's been a playwright, stage director, and film actor, and has been exhibiting his visual art for a decade or so. You don't need a complete knowledge of his works to see that his novels mark him as the nearest thing we have to an inheritor to the Burroughs strain in American fiction. That's the strain that breaks or simply ignores middle-class taboos; embraces narcotics and all kinds of sex; takes an interest in the uglier emotions, like disgust, shame, and hatred; applies actual pressure to American myths (the Western, the P.I., the gangster); has recourse to science fiction and narrative fracture; keeps its eye on the varieties of societal control (family, state, corporation, media); and doesn't shy away from anything that might be mistaken for sin."

—Christian Lorentzen, *New York*

"Indiana, a playwright, art critic, artist, and novelist with the sensibility of a rogue private investigator, is edgy in two or three ways. He's hip and unchill; he's lived on the edges of a lot of things, like fame and Los Angeles."

—Sarah Nicole Prickett, *Bookforum*

"For a time, he was comfortably categorizable: an inheritor, perhaps, of early Burroughs or John Rechy or Alexander Trocchi, or a 'fixture,' as journalists like to say, among the writers and artists who congregated around Manhattan's East Village in the 1980s . . . Now, most of the downtown luminaries are dead; a few got rich—which in artistic terms is often the same thing—but, like his own apartment building, 'an architectural pentimento' of grimmer days holding out against the metastatic luxury of condos, boutique hotels, fancy eateries, and NYU dorms, Gary Indiana is still there, developing the vivid ire and grit of his early works into a sulfurous dissection of the American character that has few if any rivals."

—Adrian Nathan West, *The Baffler*

RENT BOY

GARY INDIANA

McNally Editions

New York

McNally Editions
445 Albee Square West,
Brooklyn, NY 11201

ISBN: 978-1-946022-52-3
E-book: 978-1-946022-53-0

Design by Jonathan Lippincott

3   5   7   9   10   8   6   4

For Lynne Tillman

por•nog•ra•phy, *n* [Gk *pornographos*, adj., writing of harlots, fr. *porne* harlot + *graphein* to write; akin to Gk *pernanai* to sell, *poros* journey] 1: the depiction of erotic behavior (as in pictures or writing) intended to cause sexual excitement 2: material (as books or a photograph) that depicts erotic behavior and is intended to cause sexual excitement.

If I allow people to despise me, they should at least be good enough to say, that that is all I can do for them.

—Magdalena Montezuma,
in *The Death of Maria Malibran*

Life is very precious, even right now.

—Werner Schroeter

RENT BOY

Saturday night. A famous writer comes into the Emerson Club with his wife and another couple. He's already drunk and before they even order dinner he starts insulting his friend's wife.

"The trouble with Joanie is, Joanie's a cunt."

"Quite, Roger."

"And in that cunt, she's got the teeth of a great white shark."

"Whatever you say, old boy."

Famous Roger stews for a second in his bile. There's a champagne bucket next to the table. A crisp linen napkin looped through the handle. He wants a refill.

"A lot of people don't know anything about the French Revolution."

"How true, Roger."

"Do you know who the Jacobins were?"

"Haven't a clue," the man says.

"Well, actually, Roger, I do," Joanie says.

"You think you know who the Jacobins were."

"I don't think I know, I do know."

"Let's hear your opinions about the Jacobins, Joanie."

A beat.

"Wouldn't you rather hear my opinion of you?" Joanie is screaming. She throws down her napkin and starts to get up. "You're a *shit*. Boorish, pathological, narcissistic, and—excuse me, Diane"—she says to the writer's wife—"you had your best years a long time ago."

There was a threatening silence at the table. Joanie half-standing, trapped inside the banquette. Their faces all looked waxy, like actors in a Vincent Price movie.

"Well," Roger said, dipping his head. His silver curls caught the light. "Nobody's perfect."

All four of them roared at that one.

Another writer who shows up nearly every night is Sandy Miller. She's always in the club waiting for somebody. She has one of those leather Filofax kits she's always zipping open and shut, and a very expensive fountain pen, scribbling away. She sits at one of the tiny round tables in the front awaiting her prey. Usually she's got a small bottle of mineral water in front of her. She sips her water and writes in the Filofax, in itty-bitty handwriting that looks like a secret code. She gets in a paragraph or two while she's waiting.

Sometimes she's with a cheese. I know all the cheeses, because they come in here with other people. But, a lot of times, it's these nondescript young guys in suits. If you listen closely they turn out to be editorial assistants, people with unimportant jobs at the magazines. You can tell they're real excited about being in the Emerson Club. Gives them the feeling they're shinnying up the ladder. Sandy cultivates a lot of these guys. She also acts like I'm a great friend of hers. She calls me by my name—Mark, the one I use here—and sometimes, if I'm on a break, if she's waiting for somebody, she invites me for a drink, which I'm allowed to do here, because the image of the Emerson Club is hip. No class distinctions, right? After all, the waiter could turn out to be a writer or a movie star or something important a little further down the road. The people you meet on the way up, etcetera.

They have rooms upstairs the members can rent if they're passing through town. I'm off before two in the morning when they stop serving food, but people on the finishing shift say there's a little prostitute action going on here. I'm not sure who turns tricks. Maybe Xavier, this Spanish kid. I guess they turn a blind eye. The management, I mean. Not that Sandy Miller would ever avail herself of a waiter if she had to pay.

I read one of Sandy's books. It was all my cunt this and my cunt that for two hundred pages, stick your big dick in my cunt sort of stuff. But literary, you know. One minute Sandy's getting banged by an Arab Negro and the next minute she's a sixteenth-century pirate on the high seas, or Emily Brontë or something. Her writing is real modern. Anyway, she's always telling me she was just on television or in *Women's Wear Daily* and what a drag it is being so famous. "The only reason people know me is they've seen me on television," Sandy complains.

Tonight she dined with a woman her own age, which I guess must be forty-two. A good-looking woman. Not as made up as Sandy. Sandy wears scads of jewelry in her ears and on her fingers and this fuck-me-right-this-minute lipstick. I'm like not into women at all but even I have fantasies about Sandy's mouth wrapped around my hard virile member and shit, go figure. Her clothes always look like space outfits with shoulder wings and massive collars. Sometimes her head looks like it's trapped inside some giant tropical plant. That's outerwear. Then she slides off the Gaultier jacket, showing off a top with one shoulder bare so you can see her tattoo, one of her many I should say, which is bunches of flowers intertwined with a dragon or maybe it's a snake.

Sandy gets as much press on her tattoos and her weird clothes as she does on her books. She keeps adding more tattoos, as if she's completing this giant jigsaw puzzle. The little underground magazines love running pictures of her. Serving her and the other woman drinks I kept imagining Sandy's back looking like a diorama in the Natural History museum. I saw a book where they showed these skins taken off people in Japan who were totally tattooed. Gangster skins, because the gangsters there get tattooed all over. Their skins were preserved by some collector of rare tattoo designs. I don't want to think about how he came by them. Maybe Sandy thinks if she gets enough of them they'll skin her after she croaks and put her under glass where everybody who ever fucked her will have to look at them and think about her.

Sandy's cool but waiting on her is no picnic. She invariably wants something special, or something substituted, or fidgets for ten minutes mulling over the wine list, like she knows something about wine. Every time I've waited on Sandy Miller, she's ordered the worst wine we've got. You pour her a little, she declares that it's piquant, or woody, or, what's the word she uses, oakey. Hmm, she says, it's a touch oakey, but I like that, don't you? Also, she always wants a word with David Humphreys who owns the place, what glory would it be to just sit in the Emerson Club quietly and eat her dinner, no, she's got to have tub-of-lard Dave Humphreys dance attendance on her because she's a cheese. The sick part is, David loves to do it. Anybody famous, David comes prancing out of the kitchen full of lusty repartee. They usually talk about Sandy's cunt. So-phisticated. One night she was shouting so the whole place could hear, "My cunt is FAMOUS, they're gonna make my cunt a NATIONAL MONUMENT."

It didn't take me long on this job to figure out that Sandy acts like we're all great friends, one happy family, so she can stiff me and everybody else on tips. She even does it when she isn't paying, tells the person picking up the check to take some money back. Only rich people do that, but Sandy whines all the time she hasn't got any money, her publishers screwed her, it seems she gets screwed on every deal she makes. Added to how much she gets screwed oth-erwise, Sandy's life must be one big screw. When people come to Sandy, her supplicants, like these third-assistant editorial types, she divides the bill. I've seen her bitch over one little cognac somebody else had: "I'm not going to pay for your bad habits, sweetie." Sandy doesn't drink, only wine.

After work I took a cab up to Show Palace. Matt Hartman the porn star bumped around onstage for five minutes, rubbing his dick inside a leopard-skin jockstrap. At the end of five minutes he took it out and stroked it at the audience. I thought he'd keep going till he came, but he didn't. You're not supposed to come onstage, other people would have to step in it. Next was Gino Suave, a bulky Italian guy with a fat not very long nozzle. His emphasis seemed to be on his asshole more than his prick, he kept bending over shooting his ass to the audience and wiggling it and pulling his cheeks apart with his fingers. His tits are too big or not muscular enough, although he has a nice rippled stomach. After he'd made it clear that his ass was open for business, he shifted sort of half-heartedly around to show off his partly stiff prong. It kept going soft and he'd spin around, get the asshole churning again, all the time frantically whacking off to get himself harder. His song was "Ch-ch-ch-changes" by David Bowie. "Time may change me," he finished off, wagging his hard-on. He had this shit-eating grin on his face. "But you can't change time."

Ricky Chester also did a number. The Pogues, "Rain Street," you had to give him credit. Ricky Chester has the biggest, blackest dick I've ever seen, which believe me is saying something. He's one of those people who's always hard. He doesn't care who he makes it with, either. Six foot two, maybe a hundred eighty pounds, nice proportions. Ricky Chester has a nice face, too, kind of long and soulful. He doesn't smile while he's dancing. Mainly he stares down at his dick, like maybe it'll fall off if he doesn't keep an eye on it. He has a face you'd see on a sexy UPS deliveryman. Which is what Ricky used to do for a day job.

Ricky's dance was pretty basic. First he shucked everything but his Nikes and sweat socks and bumped around in this purple cache-sexe for a minute or two, then eased off the fig and got a bottle of lube out of his gym bag—lemon-flavored love oil, I saw the tube—squeezed some onto his penis and whacked himself off until the prick was bone-hard and glistened like a cop's rubber truncheon. He stood there pushing out his pelvis and pushing and pulling a set of make-believe hips with his fists in front of him, the whole time making faces like he's getting more and more turned on. The way he moved, you could picture some bent-over guy's ass sucking in Ricky's prick with an aria of little farts. Then he stepped down into the audience, mostly the guys in the seats against the rear wall, squatting down in their faces to give them a close-up while they slipped twenty-dollar bills into his socks. I went out and did a joint in the toilet. This middle-aged guy at a urinal jacked himself off in a bored way. He kept checking me out while I slouched against the wall, waiting for an invitation. He says:

"How you makin' it?"

I toked on the joint and just nodded, like, "Fine." The guy zips himself and stands there, nodding and swaying a little. I tried not to focus on him too vividly. He looked about fifty. Glasses. Square jowly face. Yellow windbreaker. Things went real quiet in there. The guy turns his back on me and starts rinsing his hands in the sink.

"You a performer?" He wiped his hands on the filthy pull-towel and watched me in the little mirror on the towel dispenser.

That bathroom has orange walls, a color that will drive you crazy. I shook my head.

"Not, like, here," I said. "I'm not a dancer, if that's what you mean."

He turned around and looked at me. Now he had a smirk growing in one corner of his mouth.

"But you do, um, perform? Private shows?"

Yeah, I thought, I sure do. I turned on the "suck me real good and I'll perform the Ring Cycle in your rear auditorium" smile. This guy attracted me about as much as a plate of cold spaghetti but I could see he wasn't the demanding type. Plus, this type of work, you learn to read people inside out in three minutes. Unless you're on crack. Then it takes one minute, but you're often wrong. He looked tame. Just a nice soft not too old geezer crumbling like camembert inside his windbreaker.

We went out to the lobby and sat on a bench. Boys paraded back and forth, some of them dancers who'd put their clothes back on. The guy's name is Quentin Something. He told me the last name but I forget. I said I didn't normally hang out at Show Palace. I said my rates were a lot higher than the Show Palace merchandise. Which they are. Not a problem, he says, if we decide to party. He's been saving up for a little fun, he says. As he's indecisive I ask him, "You look slightly Italian. Do you have some Italian in you?" "Me, no, I'm Irish," he says. So I say, "Well, you want some?"

So this Quentin Something's place is in the East 50s on that little street under the Roosevelt Island cable car, in the building next to the Eileen Ford Agency. Five rooms, third floor, swank. There's a piano bar for aged fairies on that block where I hustled for a few months several years ago. You go in there any night and you'll see about twenty old queens, all fabric designers and hairdressers, egging on this sixty-five-year-old fag hag at the Steinway singing "Send in the Clowns" or "The Ladies Who Lunch." Quentin struck me as a guy who'd milled around that piano plenty of nights with a gut full of gin, choking up at certain key verses of these old show tunes. Like where Elaine Strich goes, "Everybody d-i-i-i-e-s!"

He fixes me a Bloody Mary and watches me drink it while talking about his Life. That was boring enough for me to start thinking about the dome structure of the Hagia Sophia in Istanbul, which we're being tested on in class next week. All the time he sucked my cock the top of his head kept blending in with these pictures of the Hagia Sophia dome, which I hope I live long enough to see in real life instead of this old queen's Hair Club transplants.

Bruce the Pooch loves bouncing around his studio like he's that Annie Leibovitz photographer in *Perfect*, Red Hot Chili Peppers blasting out of his Aiwa speakers, three regular assistants scrambling around, taking calls, running out for coffee, setting up *la table*, as he jokingly calls it, adjusting his silver umbrella, trying different fabrics under the food. This week we're doing Christmas Treats for a start-up competitor of Gourmet.

You can't believe the stuff we use to get the color just right, like hotdog relish for a lime glaze on a tartine, or clear nail polish on a Christmas turkey to give the skin exactly the right sheen, and this afternoon, right, Bruce needed a plate of *fudge*, chocolate fudge with walnuts, we tried this, we tried that, we sent an assistant to five different places to *buy* fudge, and none of it looked right, and Bruce, who's constantly getting enemas from his slave master uptown, didn't even think it was anything odd to ask who needed to take a shit and what they ate for lunch. So guess whose turd is in the centerfold of *Cuisine* as part of the holiday magic. I got so fucked up on Bruce's coke that I ended up in Cats, against my better judgment, trawling for some sentimental type with lots of cash who'd be, like, fighting off memories of happier days at the sight of all the Yuletide decorations.

One person who hangs around Cats is called Frankie G. This is a weird little person who's had a female-to-male sex change. Her tits are flattened out in a strange way even though they're still there. She also has a lot of dopey tattoos on her arms and across her upper chest, the kind of tattoos guys in prison give themselves with a pin and a bottle of ink. Real crude drawings, letters spaced all wrong, like they can't get anything halfway artful in the joint, except Frankie isn't in the joint, so it makes you wonder. Plus, you'll enjoy this, I got a look at Frankie's "cock" one night, not up close or anything but from across the room, never mind where, kind of like a knob of sheep fat with a roll of extra gristle near the top where the cock head's supposed to be. I guess they can't graft erectile tissue or maybe nobody was willing to donate any to Frankie's cause. She looks like somebody who would probably be difficult with friends. She's got a very broad moustache but it's all wispy, like a glue job, also some strange hair growing on the sides of her breasts, like she's turning into a werewolf or something. She struts around like a guy, smokes a cigarette like a guy, hunches over the jukebox like a guy. The only thing is, the guy she's impersonating must be from some really old movie like *On the Waterfront* or that one I wrote you about with Joan Crawford and Melvyn Douglas, *A Woman's Face.* Actual guys just don't swagger around that way anymore. I guess Melvyn Douglas is a bad example anyway. Frankie is ugly, there's just no other way of putting it. But there are people who really bond to Frankie's type, the self-mutilation type, who are like endlessly fascinated with the body as this hunk of meat you can do almost anything with, kind of like Bruce with his food, if you see what I mean, or Sandy Miller's tattoos, like if the doctors decided you could graft a penis onto somebody's forehead there'd be people like Frankie lined up around the block, guys who'd been trapped inside the bodies of guys with penises between their legs while all along, deep down, in their mental image of themselves, their cocks were really on their foreheads. It takes all kinds, what can I tell you. I think there have been some compassionate if edgy profiles of Frankie G. in the tabloids. And cable shows, Frankie G. is the undisputed king *and* queen of cable guests, though he doesn't usually say much. He doesn't have to, you just look at him and that says it all, somehow.

Cable sucks unless you have at least Standard Plus. Half the stations on my TV have a little box in the upper right corner with, like, bits from movies they'll show you if you call a 900 number. It turns your home into a hotel room with the flick of a switch somewhere in Hecate County. That's where I was born, Hecate County. Then you work your way around the stations as they light up on your cable box. There are like these islands of entertainment crammed together along three, maybe four consecutive numbers, and then a patch of something not so nice, Galapagos Turtles being slaughtered for some charm they make out of its fingernails in Long Beach, California, for example. You know: "The fingernails *could* be harvested without killing this endangered species, but those whose livelihoods depend on wiping out the noble tortoise say this time-consuming process would cripple the industry." So you think about that for a second or two and then decide you'd really rather not think about that at two in the morning. You want a horror picture with Karen Black, or a comedian sticking his head up his ass at the Comedy Club. Not how they're cloning rhinos in Santa Barbara to keep the gene pool active for some future time. What future time, I'd like to know. You can see how desperate America is by how many comics they've got on the spectrum of the dial, yacking about what happened to them driving into West Hollywood or how their Cuisinart will only process white vegetables. Or the hilarious differences between women and men of dating age, whatever. And the spooky preachers and that dweeb who does the self-help affirmation schtick in those horrible sweaters. He's a real case. I can see him hitting Rounds like five times in one night with the bucks he's making, lifting you into your higher self, where it doesn't matter what your physical lower half is into. I bet he knows exactly what his lower half is into, he could give you a really clear picture in four words.

Well, who doesn't like getting fucked, I'd like to know? Guys like it, girls like it, Sweater Boy whose name is Doug Caucasian or something likes it all the time to reach his higher state of self-being. Everything you desire can be yours, he tells you. You just have to lock out the bad you, the old you, the you that hangs on to things from the past that are keeping you in a holding pattern. I guess he means you should develop amnesia and go for the gold, with the help of his workshops at the Mall in Paramus, New Jersey, or wherever. Next, Katharine Hepburn in *Stage Door.* With Lucille Ball and Eve Arden and I don't know who else. One digit over, Christopher Lee in a vampire flick where Van Helsing's holy water misses Christopher Lee by a yard and then Barbara Steele or somebody really has to, like, deal with his vampirism. Janet Jackson on MTV; Metallica in a country mode on VH1. 23 some fart with a bad weave job on the floor of Congress, reading the baseball scores into the Congressional Record. There are like three other congressmen in the whole place, and they're cooling their heels, waiting to commend some second-base pitcher for saving the national honor. Or, on the other CNN channel, they're debating whether it isn't time for the death penalty to get more creative. Jeane Kirkpatrick debates Pat Buchanan: "What about souping up that lethal injection thing in Florida with some magic mushrooms or something else that will heighten the experience of execution?" "As usual, Jeane, you would rather kill with kindness than simply kill, which is quite good enough for these enemies of society and democracy as we know it. Whatever measures are implemented, I would hope they guarantee maximum pleasure for the spectators, who after all are the wronged party. For example, decapitation by chainsaw."

Now we're easing down to those all-important single-digit numbers on the dial, which are the networks and that Spanish-dubbed station. You should see *The Exorcist* in Spanish, it really works. Color tone pattern on 5. Best of *Geraldo* on 6. Some guy has rented all this airtime on 3 to show this crawly color negative video of his drive across the country or maybe it's the same stretch of highway on a loop. I can't look at that. Zip back up through the numbers, catching three minutes of a movie that had, I think, Anthony Quinn, if that's who I'm thinking of, James Mason, and Telly Savalas. I mean Michael Caine. They're in Paris. You see, like, the overhead subway and some French bread and people drinking coffee out of little cups. Michael Caine has to assassinate either James Mason or Telly Savalas, I couldn't keep it straight.

Is this enough? I could keep right on going through my dreams, people disguised as other people, mouths opening and closing on different parts of my body. And there are, you should know, shadows from a tree outside on the wall, and on the ceiling of my bedroom, like a net moving over me.

You say in your letter you want to get to a place of safety. Those are your words. I get the feeling that for you being alone doesn't matter. That's just something I've noticed when I get together with you. Sometimes you moan when I fuck you and sometimes I feel like I'm an appliance parking away at this person who's already left the room, vacated that delicious asshole of yours completely. Your asshole is sweet enough to eat, as I think I've demonstrated plenty of times. I don't mean to say you're spacey, but it's hard to read you. A lot of times when you call you make your life sound like this disaster area nobody would want to enter. Then if you smoke a joint and ease back a little, you're like this hot person.

You maybe don't remember I go to Rutgers twice a week for classes, but this afternoon an exchange student from Singapore who didn't get a design prize they were giving out took an Uzi and blew away, like, my architecture professor, the rest of the architecture department except for E. Cabot Gristle, some retired fart that nobody can stand, I'm making the name up, and four graduate students, including the one who got the prize this guy wanted. So I guess nobody gets the design prize this year. I only saw them taking the bodies out because I was late for class. Oh, the guy shot himself after he wasted the others. It was prize or nothing for him, evidently. I'm not that way, but I can view it in a certain sympathetic light.

There's blood all over the architecture building. We have the option of suspending our classes or melting in with E. Cabot Gristle's seminars. I would, like, rather go to hell. In other words I'm free for a while. Especially for gainful employment. Don't rush to the phone if this sounds like a hustle.

When I did Wylie? In your letter it says he wouldn't admit making it with me but you could tell he had. I'm very interested in that. Some people can tell right off if two people have slept together, and some people are in their own worlds and only see what they expect to see in other people.

I'm surprised you have this vibration, if that's what you call it. I don't mean that insultingly. I just mean how in the ten seconds when I ran into you and Wylie coming out of Cats you figured out that I did him once. More than once.

Wylie has that image of very aloof very in control but once you've got him chained to an immovable object he turns into a whole different personality. More docile than you would picture. Wylie adores pain. But the best part with Wylie is verbal. He's got several scripts he's written, you can read from them while putting him through his paces like a good dog. In one script Wylie's a Nazi spy being worked over by queer CIA agents after World War II. In another one he's a parish priest who's murdered a little girl. You have to hit him and hit him. None of this is true, I'm making it up. Wylie likes to play dead. That's the only thing doggy about Wylie. Lies there like a vast white worm that splits in half at the bottom where there's a little hole. I swear it's like death in there because Wylie has, like, no reaction. Even when he's a little shitty down there the shit smells cold like something metallic instead of shit.

I got off on a tangent last time. New professors at the school. They'll probably think twice before handing out any awards for a while. We're looking at the structures of Bergamo, which are charming, but so what?

Another night at the Emerson Club. The usual lineup of gargoyles, plus Sandy Miller, who says she's about to sign a contract for a bodybuilding book. She works out twice a day. She's a shrimp, but I guess her muscles are superdeveloped. I know one set of muscles that's got to be pumped to the max, anyway.

Tonight she had two dreary people in tow, this nothing couple Sandy said own all the retail book outlets in malls in New Jersey. I defy you to find a single Sandy Miller novel in New Jersey, it just isn't going to happen. Maybe if Sandy wrote realistically about her cunt and everything that goes into it she'd have something they could sell in New Jersey, but the heroine would have to be a Mafia princess or own a big department store or have a story, at least, that would make you care about her cunt. In Sandy's books it just floats around all on its own from century to century, country to country, sucking up penises in its travels.

Sandy says her books are like commentaries on capitalism and stuff, not just about her cunt. Well, who am I to judge? She had a house salad and these quenelles of pork with raisin sauce. The couple was fawning all over her. The guy starts ordering champagne, festive occasion, evidently, meanwhile Sandy and the wife inch closer and closer on the banquette, nuzzling. Probably Sandy's giving out a little lezzie action with the wife, and they'd go back to the townhouse and the guy could watch. Sandy likes these complicated scenarios with husbands and wives and probably domesticated animals for all I know, it keeps things interesting, which is half the battle. Fucking bores me to tears half the time. I'd rather be eating ice cream.

All night it seemed that Xavier wanted to tell me something but he didn't get to it until we were going off our shift. We were in'the employees' dressing room changing out of our formals and he unrolled a magazine from his gym bag. Danny, he says, look at this. He flips through the mag, which is like *Torso* or *Mandate*, come to think of it was *Uncut*, until he comes to a spread where he's kneeling on a locker room bench with football pads and a numbered sweatshirt on, but nothing below except a pair of white socks. He looked real hot. In the picture his expression was definitely dreamy, bedroom-brown eyes staring at a point behind the camera. On the following pages he was posed this way and that way, sometimes in the sweatshirt, then without the sweatshirt but with the pads on, then nothing but the socks. Sometimes he was looking at the camera, sometimes he looked at himself with a certain surprise, like it got even bigger when he wasn't looking. His big hard-on had a slight inward curve. In the full-page first picture the tip of his cock head peeked demurely out from the rolled circle of his foreskin, later it emerged in stages until you could see the long side of it was this elegant parabola with a dramatic, sensitive-looking rim. The shaft had one slightly raised vein where Xavier was fully hard. His body looked perfect. The cock by itself was something else. But him, nice. Smooth, just the right muscle tone everywhere, nice ab definition, and still slenderish. He kept complaining that they hadn't put enough makeup on his ass zits, I could see that, but I mean, who cares? It's the kind of ass people impale themselves over, or I guess on, zits and all. You think I look good? Sexy? Is my cock big enough? He sounded really insecure about it, he wasn't just fishing for a compliment. I said the way they shot it his cock looked gigantic, of course they shoot it with the cock closest to the lens, I've seen Xavier's cock while we were changing clothes and it's, I don't know, party size, but in the photos it's a lot bigger.

He says he got paid $500 for the shoot. That's not a lot of money but it's not a lot of work, is it? I guess if he ever ends up a movie star he'll have these pictures dredged up and printed in the tabloids, with black lines blacking out his pride and joy, but otherwise, what has Xavier got to worry about? It's good advertising, really. I'm positive he's on the game, he told me. Guess what, that famous writer I wrote you about, Roger, likes getting handcuffed and pissed on and worshipping Xavier's toes. Xavier's your type, if you want me to put a word in.

Lately I'm very restless as if there was something eating away at me but I can't pin it down to anything. It's like I want to *be there*, and when I picture where *there* is, I just see some nightclub full of kids dancing and smoking dope, and in this picture I have, it's like I'm leaning my head back and have my face turned to the ceiling and somebody's filming me in a tight close-up with this look of rapture on my face. Just like Malcolm McDowell at the end of *O Lucky Man!* The longer I keep this picture in my head the stupider it looks to me, I hear clapping and stuff and voices going, Da-NEE, Da-NEE, Da-NEE, like I'm this superstar, and then I break into my really tight M.C. Hammer dance number, and finally the image fades and I'm in my bedroom smoking hash with the lights out, and the Arab kid from Domino's is kind of curled up between my legs with half of my dick in his mouth, giving me a really lame blowjob that feels like tickling. Sometimes I have absolutely no sensation in my penis anyway, I'm sure it's from using it so much in situations I'd really rather not be in. This kid has a nice body but I don't engage with it at all, except his asshole, which looks like an embossed star or something. Tonight I can't fuck him for very long and stay hard, so every few minutes I pull out and work three fingers in there with a rotary motion that he responds to. His name's Mohammed, from Saudi Arabia or someplace. He says back in his own country guys only get fucked when they're real little and when they grow up they're supposed to, you know, do the fucking, and it's considered unmanly for a guy in his twenties like Mohammed to get off on getting fucked. Besides which it's against Islamic law and they have to sneak around or get beheaded for sodomy.

On my bedroom wall I've fixed a long rectangular mirror, so we can both see the dick going in and out and stuff. Except you can't see anything in this light, and Mohammed is nearsighted, so without his glasses on it's probably a blur. We're just two vague mammals humping.

I got totally fucked up last night with Chip. There's something drew me to Chip the first time I saw him I can't put into words. It was a long time ago. I was working the toilets in the Port Authority. Or as Chip calls it the Port of Authority. Both on the game but strange to say we went home and fucked each other and we've had this intense relationship ever since, not all the time, Chip's mysterious, he comes and goes in and out of people's lives. One time I heard he was being kept in maharaja style by some pansy on upper Park Avenue, another time this kid named Fat Paul told me Chip was living in a refrigerator crate in that park on Mulberry behind the Tombs.

Chip looks a little bit the way Tony Danza used to look on *Taxi*, before he got all fat-assed and bullnecked. He's my age, twenty-five, and he's been a whore since he was sixteen. So there isn't much he doesn't know about the strange desires of other men. Chip has always got a scheme that will get him out of whoring, once and for all, only he doesn't know shit about anything besides what people want in bed and these plans always fall through.

Anyway, last night we started in Rounds and worked our way downtown. The only thing going in Rounds was this old number who looked like a toad offering fifty dollars if he could lick my feet in his car, which he'd parked in a lot down the street. Chump change. On the way to Tunnel Bar, Chip said he did the foot thing with this number once upon a time, and it isn't just licking, the guy gets you all turned on and then wants you to stuff your toes up his ass. All for fifty dollars in a fucking parking lot.

I can just picture getting busted: half your foot is up the john's hole, Gee, officer, he said he lost his car keys and I didn't want to use my fingers, it's so unsanitary. Plus, Chip said, the guy's got an old saggy ass like a pair of giant chicken wattles, and the time Chip partied with him, Chip's toenails punctured the guy's rectum and all this blood came out. Blood, Jesus. Who knows what's been up that ass, probably all the dicks in Cats who like hate using rubbers and really cream when the customer pays them extra to take it off. For the *feeling* of it, right? Then you see those guys a year later weighing ninety pounds and pretending they've never been healthier. I know one black dude with fucking lesions all over his back and he tee's the dumb johns it's his natural coloration, some kind of pigment disorder. They want to believe it, probably they beeped him at one a.m. and got him all the way up to Madison and Eighty-Seventh and they know anybody they get after that's gonna be pretty fucked-out meat.

The really gorgeous guys, everybody wants them, and this is all about scoring, right? Getting that cash in the bank or under the mattress. So even a choice item like Matt Hartman will do three four outcalls in six hours. Maybe Matt Hartman can keep it hard through all that, I don't know. The trick is not to come. But some johns want you to come, it shows you enjoyed it supposedly. I think Matt Hartman works through an agency, so you figure half what he takes in goes to them, so, four clients at a hundred and fifty a pop only comes out to three hundred dollars. For one scene in a porno movie you make three hundred dollars. Anyway, after midnight you either get a great-looking dude who's so fucked out he needs a half-hour blow job just to get semi-hard, or some skank crackhead who couldn't get a date with a blind fizzhead.

Anyway, we went to Tunnel Bar, wall-to-wall young pretty white boys in "Science Equals Depth" T-shirts, where right away I glom that everybody is talking the gay talk. How can I put it, a lot of insular types of conversations are going on. Chip and I stand at the bar and right next to my ear, somebody's talking real loud about how *as usual, these straight white males* have fucked over the gay community, like, he's *tired,* this guy, of all this homophobia, and Hollywood and the media like *have to respond* in some meaningful way and like *address the existence* of gay people, and that's why, in his column, he's exposing these closet faggots at the major studios for what they are, blah blah blah. I look at this guy, who's talking louder and louder, mainly I think to get attention from some guy standing behind the two guys he's talking to, and I swear to you he looked exactly like a pig. I mean a real pig, on a farm. I mean, they wouldn't let a mug like that within a mile of a studio unless they were making an agricultural documentary, so how would he know who's queer in the movie business. Every time I go to Tunnel Bar there's some asshole like that kind of dominating the front part of the bar, talking real intellectual but also as if they invented sexual desire, and you can tell from listening they don't know jack shit about any of it. Chip calls them the Theoretical Queers.

But Chip has his own queer theories. We went to an Indian place on Sixth Street for dinner, and Chip started in with how he thinks gay people are actually superior because they don't reproduce, they aren't "breeders," they don't add to the mess. "Do you believe in God? I don't," he said. "So if there's no God, and we just go into nothingness when we die, what's wrong with killing people?"

"Right now," I said, "we're eating all these dead animals. I'm kind of against that, but I was brought up on meat."

"Yeah, but you didn't tell me, Danny, what's wrong with killing people?"

"Well, like, if you don't *know*, Chip . . ."

"No, but all right, tell me."

"Technically," I said, "I guess it's just unfair. You go on living but you take somebody else's life away from them."

'Yeah, but life isn't fair anyway."

"No," I agreed.

"Well," he said, "how do people get to that point, do you think? Or how do they *not* get to that point? I mean, let's say you do it for your personal advantage. Everybody knows somebody that they'd be better off if that person was dead, right?"

I tried to think of somebody in my own life.

"Like a wife, or a father, something like that," Chip said.

Actually, there isn't anybody in my immediate surroundings whose death would, you know, enrich me.

"That guy in Milwaukee," Chip said. "Man, what was going on in that guy's head?" He meant that Dahmer cannibal guy, who I could see any number of aging gentlemen in Rounds going home with, no questions asked.

"Yeah," I said. "That was pretty heavy. I guess he had some kind of amateur theatrical scene going on."

"Sure," Chip laughed. "Dinner theater."

I didn't know if I wanted to go on with that because I was just putting a piece of meat in my mouth.

"Painting the skulls," Chip said. "That's what got me. Him painting the skulls all silver like trophies, where does shit like that start?"

I couldn't answer him. On some level, J., I know exactly where shit like that starts, I remembered when I was about ten or eleven and my father turned into a monster every weekend with his booze, times that I really almost pushed myself to the point. He had a shotgun in the hall closet and I thought, just one fucking blast through his heart and this could all be an ugly memory, I'd never hear his fucking fizzhead voice braying through the night anymore. I don't know what stopped me, either. It wasn't the idea of going to prison. I guess I thought about how freaked my mom would be. Then, sometimes, I wanted to kill her too. The way they set it up, sometimes he'd drive her nuts and you'd want to kill him, then another day she'd drive him crazy and you'd want to kill her. I could see neither one could control themselves, he just had to rag her and she just had to rag him, you're nothing but a shit, I've wasted all these years on you, all you like to do is torture me, blah blah blah, they could keep it up forever even though it was stupid, the whole fucking deal. You felt like you were inside this insane machinery and there was no way to turn it off.

Now that he's dead I feel some compassion for my father. But you know something, I wouldn't wish him back, not ever. My mom says she misses him, and I know it's true, but in a lot of ways she's better off. He was in a big rage most of the time.

Chip hates his dad. He talks about thumbing home to Alpena, Michigan, or wherever he comes from and running his dad over with his own truck. "Put an end to his miserable life," is how Chip puts it.

Trick book, well of course, marked according to specialty: digs urine, scat, light bondage, dirty underwear, cock ring, dildo, poppers, or, say, drag queen, foot freak, passive anal (I only do passive anal, I mean *I* do the active anal, except with Chip), suck job only, then the more esoteric ones, like the guy who gets himself off while I rub his bald head with my balls and he watches the whole thing in the mirror. If business falls off I will phone certain people. I don't like to do this. Most people know when they want to get laid and when they don't, and some of them freak if they get a call from a rent boy. It's like, who the fuck do you think you are calling me, I'm the one that calls *you*. But quite often you can put the idea in their head that they want it. I should make a notation, *extra horny*.

I tend to remember that anyway. I don't talk dirty on the phone, it's cheap. Just hi how are you I've been thinking about you, who knows, maybe they've been going in for a little variety and hitting a lot of bad meat on the trail. The only numbers I keep in the trick book are, like, guys the sex was pretty good with. Satisfied customers. Sometimes I'm wrong about that. I phoned one guy and he screamed at me for twenty minutes about how I'd done this and that he didn't like. "I don't *like* being called a cunt-ass while I'm being fucked, I told you verbal but that isn't what I *mean* by verbal. I wanted you to say something like, 'My dick feels great when I'm fucking you.'" Which is like too many words all at one time, as far as I'm concerned. "And then when I wanted you inside me, just as I was about to come, *you fucking pulled out and went soft*," he said.

Chip and I have been doing trios lately with some of our more adventurous tricks. The high rollers. Chip has an endless list of johns that like it from the front and rear simultaneously, it's less work for both of us in a lot of ways: if one loses his hard-on he's got a backup. Chip never seems to have that problem, but I do. Like I'll be doing a john real sensual and everything and suddenly my mind goes off to something funny that happened in the street, or I'll all of a sudden be seeing the, you know, scenario from outside myself, like I'm floating on the ceiling looking down at some fashion designer's rosebud gyrating on the end of my prick and the whole thing becomes a total riot. If I feel I'm about to lose the hard I start fucking real mean, making the john squeal for mercy—I mean for real, really hurting. Like I'm getting off on this so much I can't stop and I can't slow down 'cause that wet hole is making me *crazy*, ride that stiff meat, pussy-ass, here I come. You know I have a fairly awesome piece, not to brag about it, and it stabs like hell if you jam it in hard, pull it out and jam it in again, whack whack whack, because it's real wide as well as long, and then it's like the *trick* says he can't take any more, his rectum's gonna explode, please stop, so I pull out and then it's on him that we stopped. You know. "Oh, man, I was fuckin' you so good, fuckin' that hot ass of yours with this big dick, shit, take a look at this, this is sad. That cock won't get hard again 'less you suck it, baby. Suck it like you're in love with that big dick." Nine out of ten occasions they're all sucked out by that time and kind of on to the next subject in their heads, like whether they can get you dressed and paid for and out of there in time to catch the end of the late movie or *The Robin Byrd Show*, so they'll pop a few inches of it into their mouths and work it long enough to be polite and then start straightening out the ashtrays.

Anyway, it takes the pressure off when you've got two studs, because it's like the john is outnumbered, right? And it's harder for him to complain that he isn't getting satisfied (not that many do), and maybe he's also just a little scared.

Like what's to stop us from choking him to death with a Pratesi pillowcase and picking over his swank apartment for souvenirs. You don't always know what you're walking into on the other end, either, especially if they call you from an ad. I've known guys that get real sick in the head, like they have to make you feel like a piece of shit and remind you forty-seven ways that you're only a penis for sale, mainly because they feel guilty about the whole situation. Like it's a big comment on how pathetic they are that they have to pay to get laid. That's not the majority. Strangely enough, most of the ad-answering johns are practically my own age, a little older, a lot of them wouldn't have to buy it if they went out and cruised the bars or whatever. They're usually not bad looking. Sometimes on the plain side. I think it's mainly that they don't want things to be emotional. They don't want to have to cope with a lot of messy feelings.

Christmas break. I'm getting used to writing you these letters. It's making me see some things, I guess. I'm doing all right grade-wise, since you asked. I can't decide between landscape architecture and "real" architecture, which takes years longer to learn. Between the life of hustling and everything else there is a kind of invisible barrier. I mean even my close friends don't know I do this. The hustling takes you into a different world. I guess Chip is a friend but I don't trust him, you know? Because he's a hustler. He has that hustler head. Everything's a short-time con. If the customer talks too much, Chip just cuts to the chase: "You wanna suck my big piece tonight? You want my luscious prong to love your asshole good and hard or you wanna tell me the rest of what happened during your busy day? You decide, man, I got a lot of people waiting on this great big thing here." Chip has a way with words, but he's really fucked up. Like he's got eight inches, maybe, but he'll tell the client nine and a half, and some people actually can tell the difference right away. An inch can be a pretty big thing in this business. On the other hand nobody ever complained about Chip's eight inches once they had it in them. But still. I've seen Chip agree on a price with a client and then mooch all kinds of other shit out of them once he gets to their place. Or: "It's only this much the first time, next time it'll be cheaper."

Some of that money craving comes from doing dope. That's where Chip got his name, he chips. Not real bad, he'd never get it up if he had a big habit. But it causes problems. One time I set him up with one of my best johns, a guy named Kevin on Sixth Street. Kevin isn't rich, his money comes and goes. But he's a nice guy, good-looking, too. When he's flush he blows it on sex. He's one of the few clients I can talk to about anything real, besides you. He's a music composer and I think he's either really talented or really committed to the delusion that he is. He like glommed a look at Chip one night in Trix, Chip was playing the *Terminator 2* video game in the front, so I introduced them. About a week later Kevin asks me all this stuff about Chip, what's he like, what's his attitude, would I arrange a date, etc. He really liked Chip, he didn't even ask how big his endowment was. So Chip goes over to Kevin's rat hole on the Lower East Side, right? And Kevin cooks him a whole chicken dinner, lays it out real nice on the kitchen table but naturally Chip wants to eat it on the bed, after they eat they watch a movie, not a porn movie but a regular movie, and this is all, like, to make Chip feel he's being treated like a friend instead of a whore, so they do it, finally, and then Chip asks him for fifty dollars extra, because he's spent so much time there. Plus he leaves his socks on, so Kevin really feels like he's doing it in the backseat with a twenty-dollar hooker. And afterwards Chip brags to me about it, "I fucked your friend up the ass without a rubber on," like, he took the rubber off when Kevin had his back turned. Okay, Kevin figured that out after a few minutes but by then, you know, he was in the throes and his judgment was fucked up. The only real intelligent part of Chip is his penis, getting it up there raw is unbelievable. Send you through the ceiling. I said, You asshole, what about AIDS, and Chip goes, Shit, man, the guy fucking don't get AIDS, it's the one's getting fucked. That's bullshit, man, I said, but even if it's true, what if you've got it, you'd be giving it to him. Yeah, well, he says, tough shit. If I've got it they can all have it.

Chip's living in the Martha Washington. I had a room there for about two years before I found this place. They keep it up but it's your basic dump full of junkies, junkies and transients. You can bet there's a lot of wastebaskets full of crack vials. I know these lonely hotels the way you know your father died, the little rooms the same dimensions as jail cells which makes a lot of people feel right at home, but I'm skipping jail this incarnation. I mean I've been there, once, and you can have it. Jail is drastic. Like don't even mention jail around Danny. I think a lot about the spaces people spend time in, even if I can't express it in writing. In the hotels it's a big deal to get a big room, you can tell how people are making it by the size of their rooms. Half the people are cracking up from isolation and the other half float around between nobody home and scary excitement over some controlled substance about to arrive. Quite a few harmless eccentrics in there, too. Chip's got a bed and a desk and a window on the airshaft and a little TV set, do you think he ever reads a book, no, never. Every porn magazine you can think of. I like them too but Chip *reads* them. I honestly don't know why I'm attracted to him the way I am. It's not his looks, I don't go after looks except when it's business, it's easier to fuck something you can stand looking at if you don't care about it anyway. With Chip it's something about him that's kind of defenseless. He's like a kid, completely irresponsible, anything distracts him, you could probably lead him right down the street just by flashing a bright object. Chip doesn't know how to listen to people, he just listens for his hustler opportunity. To him a potential john's all blah blah blah, he'll agree to anything and then do exactly what he pleases, fuck what they want, if they complain he sort of threatens violence. He's so simple. But there's something in there that isn't so simple. I can't put it in words.

Anyway, I went to his room last night and we drank a quart of beer together and watched shit on TV, laying on the bed, and after a while we took our clothes off, I can't describe what we did but it felt good, when we finished we laid there holding each other and I felt this strange peace washing over me like I'd taken a sleeping pill, even though some breeders in the next room were having a fight, You cheap bastard, she says, it's always gotta be your way, and he says, You fuckin' cunt, what more do you want after all I do for you, etcetera. First Joe and now Morty, every one of your goddamn family except Marcia and that's only because she married into this shit. Yeah, she says, you like Marcia so well why not go over there and stick your fuckin' prick in her yeast infection, she'd love it just to get her knife into me. But it all sounded like a million miles away. We weren't in the room anymore but someplace better than the room, a castle overlooking the sea or a cabin in the woods, someplace else, anyway.

The Hagia Sophia was built by the fourth Roman emperor, Justinian, in honor of his wife, Theodora, who happened to be a big whore. In those days, women who performed onstage were all whores and Theodora was born in a trunk, kind of a child star in the Roman theater. By the time she was ingénue age she would get dicked in each of her openings by most of the Roman Senate right up in front of the footlights and after she wore them out she took on their Nubian slaves.

Then I guess somebody took her to Constantinople, some rich john, and she made a deal with an oracle or a witch to get the Emperor to fall in love with her and marry her. Once she was the Empress she like wanted to erase her past and one by one had everybody who ever saw her "perform" put to death, hundreds and hundreds of them, plus most of the people she banged. She'd also dropped a kid somewhere along the way, and when the kid was fourteen he wanted to meet his mother so he went to Rome and announced himself and ten minutes later she had him eaten alive by starving rats.

So this temple built for a prostitute is one of the miracles of architecture in the world, covering 81,375 square feet, the largest Christian church ever constructed. Centuries after they built it Mohammed the Second turned it into a mosque. Maybe in honor of his own whore. You have to be a pretty big whore to get any type of monument built to you these days. I read in the *Post* where that giant developer, Stagpole, has to sell his shares in the Stagpole Condominium Towers, the monument he erected for *his* whore and their three kids (which probably aren't his) because his financial empire is like crumbling from within on account of the recession. What isn't. Even with all his debts, Stagpole must be one of the richest cheeses in New York, an aged Stilton among men. I've waited on him at the Emerson Club, when they threw a party for Joey and Cindy Adams. Talk about a couple from hell. Those two are *both* like Ruth Gordon in *Rosemary's Baby.* Imagine being like ninety years old and still trying to social climb. Stagpole wore these big diamond cufflinks and a tie pin with a heart-shaped yellow diamond and his whore, of course, had jewels dripping out of her hair and her dress, a big dumb blond Hungarian with that permanently surprised look they get after three or four face lifts, he'd had a few tucks here and there himself, somehow the way he kept showering his attentions on her you just knew he was getting ready to trade her in for a newer model, somebody American so he doesn't have to listen anymore to that horrible accent.

•

Three hours at the gym, pumping lats and abs and pecs, checking out my magnificent form in the wall mirrors, gulping down electrolyte Kool-Aid and carbo coolers, I look at myself through the hungry eyes of a possible client. Nothing's worse than a pimple, or that scrambled look you get from a hangover, everything has to be flawless, the hair neatly cropped around the ears and a little fussed with at the neck, posture straight and alert, all the parts of the body have to sing with health, like it's a living room johns can walk into and get comfortable in.

Half the guys pumping iron at three in the afternoon have got to be whores. There's no way that many blacks and Latinos nineteen or twenty years old have the freedom to work out all afternoon and then maybe come back at night if they're trying for special effects. You sit in the lobby of the Gaiety some time and watch the talent sit around in jock straps yacking about what they did at the gym and where there's a Body Beautiful Contest at one of the hotels. Well, that's what they've got, a body, you might as well work it while you've got it, especially if your brain is the size of a dead flashlight battery and nothing much is going to happen later on. I don't want to shock you or anything, but one of the major drags of this profession is having to talk all the time to people with low mentality. I have to strain sometimes to figure out what planet some of these guys are on. It's like their own bodies are the only things they can focus on.

The shit they eat in spite of all the working out boggles the mind. Fried shit from the Mexican's, egg foo rat and mu shu stray mongrel from the Chinks, Kentucky Fried, stinky gooey pizzas with bits of dog crap it looks like or maybe hamburger sprinkled on top. Speaking of dogs, on Fridays, Bruce the Pooch likes to snort MDA—I'd like to know where he gets it—put on *Let It Be* (not the Beatles, the Replacements) and throw a little Nightmare Food Party in the studio. Sometimes a select one or two people from outside get invited. We take everything out that we've used all week, condiments, hunks of meat, fish, piles of disgusting vegetables we've spray painted and dipped in coloring or melting oceans of rancid whipped cream, rice pilafs spiked with wood shavings and broken toothpicks, Swedish meatballs made from Alpo, and of course the food substitutes, also a lot of fun, plus Bruce's harnesses and whips and Wall of Mylar Mirrors and what have you. Stage One of this party everybody dreams up a Dish to Puke Over, which has rules, the plate has to be arranged so no one in the room would think of eating it, hopefully it's so disgusting you get dry heaves just looking at it, and then we get Bruce hitched up to one of his devices and slap food all over him, cat food and ketchup and strawberries and shredded candied sweet potatoes, whatever, somebody gets a prize for most nauseating entree, and whoever is beating Bruce when he comes has the choice of eating off the prize plate or licking off Bruce. You'd think the assistants would fuck up the torture just to avoid that but these queens are *afraid* of Bruce, Bruce is one powerful enema slave and foot worshipper in his chosen industry. It takes a tough man to be a tender chicken. Sorry. He's never squirted on my watch, but there's always a first time and I think the Friday I have to eat the Blue Ribbon Special is the Friday I quit.

Anyway, the queens at the gym. Some I recognize from the places, they smile and say hi and a lot of them are friendly with each other, maybe they dance at the same clubs after working hours. Sound Factory, Tramps, Sugar Reef. On the other hand I try and maintain a certain aloof quality because whoring, once it's generally known that you do it, people type you in a very specific way. And they feel they can talk to you like you're open for business twenty-four hours a day, regardless of where you are or who you happen to be with. Which is okay with most of the rent boys I know but not okay with me.

Trix still has a zillion Christmas decorations dripping from the ceiling, lit-up candy canes and gold tinsel along with the usual blinking red lights and that close smoky atmosphere, the really desperate cases from the Port Authority zipping in and out hoping a really blasted john will stand them a beverage and maybe overlook the fact that they obviously have no current address and their socks and underpants stink and they need a crack fix, while the better-off studs nurse their drinks at the bar or along the wall or stand posing down around the pool table. There's always a group of middle-aged queens at the bar, whooping it up with the fag hag bartender, they all have their chosen tricks they make it with and act a little bit superior to the surroundings, Trix is their regular bar. The talent cruises up the street to Cats and down again, maybe taking in a few blocks of Eighth Avenue where there's usually six dozen police cars converging on some skanky pickpocket who gets bludgeoned to a pulp while "resisting arrest" before they take him in.

Rounds also has the decorations hanging but there it's these tasteful crystal snowflakes made from plastic, dangling in exact symmetrical rows under those saw-tooth pattern mirrors in the dropped ceiling over the bar, with tiny blue Christmas lights placed just so. They drop the house lights in stages after 7 p.m., so you get that glowy burnt orange effect all through the place. I think the queen that designed that place must've looked at the Rothko Chapel in Houston. For a buyer's market. Rounds has the worst lighting I can think of. You can't really make out faces until you're up close, everything at a distance is fuzzy and vaguely threatening. Like a Rothko painting, but I mean, who wants to blow a Rothko painting?

I made the mistake of going there early the other day, get this, I walk in, and I'm, like, the only hustler. Five middle-aged guys are all clanned together at one end of the bar, snacking on these cheap appetizers. Like Rounds can't afford anything besides a handful of celery sticks and Kraft Cheddar Cheese on a tasteful little cutting board. I thought of toothless sharks gnawing at something soft and decomposing in the ocean. They all have that awful john look, sad and disgusted with life but boy are they gonna party, party and then have a heart attack, all 45–65, glasses, clothes they wore to the office, none of them fat or awful but bleary, somehow, I mean they've all gone out of their way to look real prosperous and in control, so you're supposed to think they're millionaires, not in any way desperate, more like gentlemen connoisseurs of yummy muscled boy flesh who can take it or leave it, they all know the game backward and forward and when I march into the room there's this immediate surge in the animation level, I go straight to the back lounge but nobody's there, no one in the restaurant, either, just a couple old polite drunks at the end of the bar near the piano and that clutch of gee-zers down the front, so I pass time, I phone my answering machine, there's a call from a regular, this lawyer, Chuck Vickers, wants to know can I fuck his brains out between three and four on Saturday afternoon, no problem, I amble back to the bar—how do you like that, "amble"—and plant my adorable high-priced ass at a fussy distance from everybody else.

Age doesn't bother me. What bothers me is that Rounds has all kinds of strange pretentions about it and even the rent boys have to put on an act, like, "I'm not just a hustler, I'm a screenwriter," "I'm not just a hustler, I also work for so and so designer as a model," or you have to pretend you have all these famous friends, live at a great address, whatever. Fuck, man, *nobody* is "just a hustler." It's like everybody saw the same bogus movie about Park Avenue call girls and wants to live up to that corny bohunk vision of elegance the female escort services advertise on Channel 35: "Champagne, candlelight, the better things in life. We'll help you find magic in the big city." That's why they've got that restaurant in Rounds, to complete this hokey fantasy that a date is much, much more than an old man rotating on a fresh dick for an hour. Not that a dick is that fresh by the time it gets to them, I mean like a dick they haven't had before. None of the clients dresses with any type of individual flair. Which is how you can tell very few of them are really rich, there's no personality. The johns in Rounds get very touchy about shit, they're even more fucked up than the johns in Trix because they've got the money to pay $7.50 for a drink and they still don't have Love. Or they've been chained for years to some antique-and-show-tune queen they've been foolish enough to grow old with. Some of them are married, kids, the whole thing. That can be a can of worms over dinner, too. You see much more appealing fashion statements in low rent joints like Cats. In Rounds they all try for that windswept, Martha's Vineyard, early retiree look, even when they're in Madison Avenue drag. You get the glen plaid shirts and the nylon windbreakers and the dock shoes or the suit, which in Rounds looks like Count Dracula time. The big barge pulling in to get serviced after a grueling day of kissing ass in an office cubicle. And the johns love to talk. Some of them will talk your ear off all night and then say how nice it was meeting you, maybe another time, and if you score, lots of them invite you to eat there in the restaurant with them, more talk, of course sometimes you're really hungry and it saves the cost of a meal, or the john turns out interesting, but everybody also gets a good look at what you're gonna have to fuck after dinner, while you get a jumbo dose of the john's life story. Or he wants every detail about yours. I think I've overheard a million john life stories and another million whore life stories and once you plow off the bullshit the john's story's always "I'm lonely" and the whore's story's always "I came from a dysfunctional family." It's comical how some of the hustlers work these old geezers for sympathy, they get a little choked up when they get to the part about "abusive parents." The johns have heard it before but most of them cultivate that image of Daddy, understanding older man, it helps them I guess humanize the encounter. The whores I know all come from hideous families where you hear the story and you think, "What the fuck do people even think they're doing, having kids?" I mean there's so many kids that are just gonna be born into shit and grow up with no sense in their brains, this city's crawling with them, I suppose you'd have to put Chip in that category but he's never killed anybody as far as I know. Which for me is kind of a cut-off point. I understand why people kill other people but I'm just not into it.

What I'm getting to, I'm in Rounds, and right after the lights go down the place starts filling up with talent, some of it real talent, like this gorgeous blond mute kid with his friend who talks in sign language and sometimes interprets the johns for him, he's not completely deaf but he has trouble, they say that kid fucks like a crazy condemned angel. The johns have to compensate for what he can't hear by getting real imaginative with their tongues. They say there are guys who will spend a thousand dollars for the privilege of making him come, and I bet it's worth it, he's special. In comes Rooney, construction worker from Miami, not that tall but a great sarcastic face and a terrific body, supposedly his cock's so large some customers just give up, but plenty of them find uses for it. I stay at the bar and naturally get a few geezers interested but, for some reason, tonight, I can't keep up my end of the dialogue, they're either too pathetic or too loosened up on alcohol. The rule of thumb in Rounds is never turn anybody down but I like to go in there when the savings account goes over $10,000 just so I can tell some of these creeps I'm not interested in their urgent sexual needs. Money makes money makes more money but what is money if you have to fuck everybody who asks you.

Then Chip walks into the bar. With geezer, but one look and you just knew this geezer was *somebody.* I can't explain because a lot of these johns look dignified but this guy looked embalmed. Not in a bad way, but kind of like Basil Rathbone or John Carradine, handsome skinny and over the hill, carrying himself as if nothing mattered in the world, certainly not this assortment of shabby people drawn together to kill or be killed, spiritually I mean, or anything else besides Chip, when he looked at Chip the geezer's face which you could see the skull through got more amiable and indulgent, though not stupid, which is what most of the johns look like when they're smiling at tricks, stupid. What are they smiling at? The fact that they know there will always be a museum of perfect boy bodies to worship at, and any item can be had for less than two hundred dollars an hour. Like a long long-distance phone call, really. What am I saying, it *is* a long-distance phone call. You phone your need for what you can't have through the wiring of my body. I don't mean you in the sense of *you*. But where does the call go.

Chip's geezer carries a walking stick he doesn't need and he's got soft gray leather gloves that he's taken off and holds in one withered palm. A full-length leather coat, belted, really smartly tailored, and a snap-brim black hat, round gold-rimmed glasses, he's got these quick eyes, also a kind of snide way of looking over his shoulder at noises, the whole effect of this guy was pretty awesome. Chip, I could tell, was on his best manners, really talking with this guy, they went down the length of the bar and banged a sharp right into the restaurant, I saw them getting settled in a booth, first the john took off his coat and hat and Chip brought them out to the coat check like a perfect little gentleman, though of course he had that smartass smirk on his face like he always does. At this point somebody's playing an entire Barbra Streisand album on the jukebox, a really Wagnerian cover of "Sam You Made the Pants Too Long," the old queens at the bar are shrieking along to it, I kind of intercept Chip out at the coat check and ask him who's the john. Hey, Danny, he says, how's it hanging, then his voice drops, not that anybody can hear us out in the foyer, especially over Simply Barbra and her enchanted adenoids, That guy isn't just some trick, Chip says, all sincere-like. *That* guy is my ticket out of here.

He's leaning against the dark mirrors on the wall, I can't get out of my mind how pretty Chip looked in that lighting, he had on a black turtleneck sweater that really set his face off, the black hair like some extremely rare Siberian fur. It was hard to put him together with that shitty room in the Martha Washington, he'd gone into some transformation mode, new gray corduroy slacks, sleek ankle boots, glossy haircut, I figured he was being kept by that geriatric number, and then he says, Guy wanted to check the place out, maybe have a party. Uh-huh. I've been like staying at his house, Chip says, looking around with that prickly nervous look you get a lot of in Rounds. Big place on Gramercy Park. He's a doctor. Oh wow, I say. Gramercy Park. And with a *physician*. Big time. Yeah, well, funnily enough he's taking an interest in me, Chip says, a little bit defensive I thought, or even hostile, like, "You never really took care of me," but I said great, that's great, Yeah, Chip says, you're not gonna believe this but he doesn't even want to sleep with me. I thought you said he wanted to party, I said. Yeah, but not like sex, just maybe meet some of the guys. He sees a lot of potential in me to like maybe work at his clinic in a regular job. Like as a paramedic or you know get into EMS or something. He feels kind of fatherly and protective towards me.

Well, that was new. I've known a lot of johns with fatherly protective feelings that kind of developed after a while, but never without some horny unfatherly feelings going on at the same time. When I started doing this I'd sometimes get attached to a john and think maybe I could go to them just for advice or to talk or whatever, have some regular human contact outside of the physical stuff, and, frankly, nothing doing. And once in a while a john might get fantasies about having a relationship, but let's face it, they know you're balling all these other people and maybe that's a risk they'll take when they're driven to it but ordinarily they want a nice straight settled person who isn't maybe bringing home a case of AIDS or whatever. And psychologically, too, it's not much fun, is it. Of course this doctor of Chip's is pretty elderly. Sometimes really old geezers get themselves off fondling or licking parts of your body or just watching you jerk off. Anyway, I'm not sure how wonderful it would be if you needed EMS and Chip showed up, this trick had to be pretty gone to get that scenario into his head.

Whatever the geezer's scene was, I really couldn't get into it. I don't know if it was the leftover Christmas ornaments and shit or that awful feeling when you've been in one place way too long and there's no mystery left about what the deal is, maybe it sounds strange but even in Rounds, sometimes, for a minute here and there, I can feel like something's opening up and becoming possible, a little bit beyond what's already happened to me, like the next trick's going to shake something loose that's frozen inside me, I can't explain it, but anyway, I had to get out of there. I thought about calling you, telling you I had to talk to somebody, finally I did phone you from the pay phone on the corner all the hustlers use, but you had the machine on, natch, when I got home I found a letter from you in the mailbox I haven't opened yet, and I was pissed off and sad and exhausted all at the same time. I've tried to break through with you and I know you're just using me, filing these letters into a book, up above it all.

I kind of thought if I mentioned jail you'd freak out a little. I'm not in the witness protection program or anything, if that's what you're worried about. I was in jail overnight, DWI, and then I had to see a social worker twice a week for two months and go to these rehabilitation classes and only use my car to drive back and forth to work. I had a restaurant job, it's when I was living in New Jersey.

The classes were weird. All these teenybop girls in tight skirts who'd make about fifty trips to the coffee machine with a little less clothing on every trip, shaking that moneymaker for all the so-called eligible drunk driver studs in the room, mainly greasers from Brooklyn trapped in a John Travolta time warp and a few nervous-looking guys of like forty who probably got nabbed on Ninth Avenue with some twenty-dollar snatch in the car, and once in a while they'd bring in a uniformed officer to describe some particularly hideous accident caused by driving while intoxicated. One time the cop tells us about a whole car full of Jersey teens speeding home from their senior prom, trashed out of their minds, each and every one of them an honors student, he says, with their whole life ahead of them, slam bang into a tree on a blind curve at ninety miles an hour, all killed and mutilated, under a carpet of stars. He really said that. A carpet of stars.

I'm still doing two courses during the week, French Gardens and Western Architecture, plus the dinner shift at the Emerson Club on the weekends, plus Bruce, plus hustling. Bruce is having some type of nervous breakdown which has been obvious for quite a while, he's like some holdover from the eighties with the coke and everything. A lot of Bruce's friends have like bought the farm from AIDS and I get the feeling he's worried about it or maybe he tested positive, he's waiting around to get sick, the other day he started in about the ozone hole and how the ozone hole will speed up HIV because of ultraviolet. Come to think of it the ozone hole could really screw up my career as a landscape architect. Sandy Miller told me that the Dalai Lama believes the human race will be extinct in another forty years, "he doesn't say that publicly," she said, implying that she has personal conferences with the Dalai Lama, maybe she does, maybe the Dalai Lama's a big fan of her books, with Sandy you never know. Maybe they do lunch whenever the Lama is in town or something. She used to have this thing about Richard Gere, who I guess is the official consort of the Dalai Lama. Sandy had this kind of quirky period where every time you talked to her she found a way to bring Richard Gere into the conversation, Richard this Richard that, and after a while she was mentioning Richard all the time as though they were having some wild S&M affair. You know how that is? When somebody gets a little deranged on something and constantly talks about it indirectly, like you're supposed to guess the whole story? Well, finally one night Richard Gere walks into the Emerson Club with Cindy Crawford and moves right past Sandy's table without so much as a glimmer of recognition, and from the way Sandy handled it I realized she'd never even met Richard Gere. Naturally I didn't say anything about it but the next week Sandy buys me a G&T and says real confidential, "Richard won't even acknowledge me, it's really disgusting. He used to tell me nobody fucked as good as I did, why do people get so turned around by relationships?" I thought, yeah, especially ones they don't even know about. But this episode made me really sorry for Sandy. Even with all her books and everything she still doesn't feel like she even exists. Believe me, I know that feeling. Like no matter what you do or how you try to prove yourself there's always something holding your head underwater, there's always this loneliness that drains you out while you're sleeping so you wake up wrung out with every bad thing that ever happened weighing you down. And Sandy's like really gone, she always has been, it's like she's talking right through you at her own face in a mirror, there's nobody else there.

So, I finally met Chip's new dude. And the dude's entourage. I like calling him a dude because it's the last word that would come into your brain. As I mentioned, he looks like John Carradine in *The Bride of Frankenstein*, "that strange Dr. Pretorius," and he's a doctor and everything. Chip like called my beeper and when I called back this kind of lispy young woman's voice answered, "Crathnitz Rethidenth," which sounded like a home for dogs or something, so I said, you know, "My name is Danny, somebody there phoned my beeper," thinking it was a wrong number, but then Chip's voice comes over the phone, Hey, Danny, how you doin'? Where the hell are you, I say, and it crosses my mind he's got some female type of client he can't fuck or something, needs an extra prick on the job, just what I need, fuck a cunt first thing in the afternoon. It was around five.

I'm over on Gramercy Park, he says, at that address I've been staying, I told you about Guy, I came in with him at Rounds last week, What, I said, that old number? Yeah, Dr. Crashnitz, he'd uh like to meet you, I told him how you're my best friend and everything and we're all just sitting around having cocktails, so if you're not doing anything, why not come over? Well, my first thought was, whatever's happening it's bound to be pretty sick, a doctor on Gramercy Park who wants to meet rent boys, so I said, It doesn't sound like my scene, dude. Hey, man, Chip says, we're just hanging out, havin' a few, shootin' the shit. There isn't any scene going on, if there was a scene, man, I'd like fill you in, wouldn't I?

Of course Chip is a born liar, you can hear it in his voice when he's coming on all sincere. You'll be standing next to him in a bar when he starts his routine with some trick: Oooh, man, I find you so attractive, you are really cute, man, you are turning me on. And the trick goes all skeptical: Really? You've got to be joking. No, man, a lot of the guys come in here, it's a drag, you know? But I guess maybe you don't go with hustlers anyway, right? You look too young. All the lines. Chip's been reeling them off for at least ten years, he's like a walking tape deck. But I was curious, I guess. Like I told you, I've always had a lot of complicated feelings about Chip and I suppose I wanted to see just how tired this new scene of his was. Even though I know that nothing ever really changes in his life, if I don't see him for a while I get this awful fear he's dead, or actually found the person of his dreams who's gonna make him happy and that'll be it between him and me.

I don't live that far from Gramercy Park. I've had this place on Twenty-Eighth Street for a couple of years, since I left the hotel. It's a floor-through with four rooms, kind of medium size. I did in-calls for a few months when I first moved here and then I realized it really bummed me out having customers invade my living space. Besides, the encounter is about fantasy, right? And when the trick sees where you live, what you've got on your wall, the little domestic way you're set up, that makes you into a very specific person. Too specific. One thing, you don't want to encourage fantasies that are like based too much on who you really are.

It's a quiet block. I only had to cut over to Third Avenue and down, then over on Nineteenth Street. It was one of those warm days we've been getting even though it's supposed to be winter, fluky warm so the mood of the street changes into like springtime, though the sun was going down, it was one of those houses near Washington Irving High School with wrought-iron balustrades and scads of ivy growing up the walls, red brick but with a New Orleans type of flavor, the shutters on the ground floor shut, so I walked up and rang the bell. The door opens and this

B-movie heavy's standing there, a beefy guy about six foot three in a blue double-breasted suit and a striped tie. He's got the face of an old tortoise, pitted skin, thick black eyebrows, kind of long beaky lips, black eyes, looks me over with this crumbly secretive smile and says, They're expecting you.

The guy sounded the way he looked, like a gangster, but he also had something a little prissy about him, like this was the type of guy who would get very squeamish about his nails not being manicured—anyway, there's a narrow hall as you go in, next to a polished wooden staircase, and a dim chandelier, it's pretty dusky inside, dark green wallpaper with fleur-de-lis flocking, small Barbizon landscapes in faded gilt frames, a rickety Louis Quatorze secretary where the mail's piled up with some candelabra on it, a runner carpet with cabbage roses, and a set of big doors at the end. It's very precious, very Northern European, somehow, but decayed, like a good stiff wind would smash everything to smithereens.

What I'm getting at is, this house has a definite atmosphere, a time travel feeling when you walk in, it's a different century and you feel if you looked out the window you'd see ladies in crinolines and parasols and horse-drawn carriages. The floor creaks under your feet, the doors creak, too, it's like a place that's under sedation and having slightly creepy dreams. I followed Stanley—that's the B-movie guy—down the hall to this parlor. A very long room with lots of draped windows, plus one big window that's stained glass, arabesques of stained glass with a figure in the center I couldn't quite make out because there wasn't any light coming through it, the first object you see is a Bechstein grand piano, then when you turn it's this big space full of sofas, armchairs, objects d'art of all descriptions, the guy has a goddamn Giacometti, plus a Marden painted marble, several minor Impressionists, a bronze statue of Mercury, and some of those really rare globe lamps veined with crimson, plants everywhere, paintings, a regular art gallery, with that same worn-out antique look as the hallway, and in a sort of conversation area right at the end, near the front windows, there's Chip luxuriating on a sofa with his shoes off, sipping a glass of champagne. Yo, Danny, he says, giving me a little wave, and he giggles, like it's the biggest joke.

Yo, Chip, I say, and as I get closer I notice these two other people in the room, sunk into big armchairs facing the couch: the guy from the other week in Rounds, Dr. Crashnitz, who's holding his champagne glass near his lips and staring into space broodily, in a black suit, black tie, I see also he's touched up his hair with a black rinse, he looks like an enormous raven or crow. He nods his chin without really looking at me. I flash on the fact that I have seen a million movies where crumbly old men sit in wing chairs looking just like this guy, he could be Boris Karloff or Sydney Greenstreet or Vincent Price, any of those guys, and this Stanley dude, you know, has that Eddie Constantine or Lionel Stander type of rough-hewn, burly quality. In the other chair there's this nurse. I mean in a nurse's uniform with a nurse's cap, the whole kit. Except she's got these strapless high-heeled black shoes on. The nurse has this wild blond hair packed under the cap, black at the roots, lots of eyeliner and lipstick and green eye shadow and, what can I tell you, she's hot. Slutty-looking and hot. Nice tits.

Nice shape. Since Chip's laying there with this stupid grin on his mug not introducing me, the doctor clears his throat and holds out a bony hand and says, "I'm Guy Crashnitz. And you must be Danny." I shake his hand. It feels like snakeskin. Crashnitz looks into my eyes. I look into his eyes. I don't know what I'm seeing there. Desire? Contempt? Suddenly he lurches forward and cranes around the chair wing to look at Stanley, who's just standing around with a big palooka grin.

"Get this boy a glass of champagne," Crashnitz says. Then he slumps back in the chair. "Or perhaps you'd care for something else? Whiskey? Scotch?" I stood there stupidly. Then Chip moved his feet on the couch leaving me room to sit down, so I sat. "Uh, champagne's just great," I said.

"I'm Mavis Montgomery," the nurse says, bending forward a little. Then she raises her champagne glass at a crooked angle and gives me a wink. I'm thinking Mavis is a real good-time gal, you can tell she's had plenty of cocktails already.

"Chip's told us a lot about you," she said. From the big smile on her face I got the impression she was stoned as well as drunk, and then I realized Chip wasn't saying a word, just beaming his shit-eating grin, and I figure, uh-oh, they're both on Planet Morphine. So Stanley comes waddling back with my champagne. He's got a glass for himself and I see he's put a shot of cognac in his. Stanley paces around on the carpet, never lighting anywhere, but he stops in his tracks long enough to drink the whole glass down in one gulp, then he heads back to the champagne bucket, which is way in back near the grand piano.

"Chip tells us you study architecture," Crashnitz said. "That's an interesting field."

"It sure is," Mavis crooned, slurping champagne. "I just love buildings. I mean, you look around, they're everywhere!"

"They're just adding a new wing to the hospital where I work," Crashnitz went on. "It completely blots out the view from my office windows. Quite hideous."

Mavis nodded eagerly. "We're not there that much," she said. "Even so, you feel pretty closed in when you're over there."

Chip's eyes were shut. His head rested on the sofa arm. He stretched his legs out and planted his socked feet in my lap.

"Yup," he sighed, meaning what I couldn't tell you.

"It's true we spend less and less time there," Crashnitz said, looking at Mavis.

Mavis got a thoughtful look as she watched me rubbing Chip's feet. I'd started to do it without thinking about it and it instantly gave me a hard-on.

"We have our own little clinic downstairs," she told me. "It's the best little urology lab in the city."

"I'm a kidney man," Crashnitz said.

Suddenly Stanley piped up from the vicinity of the piano: "You're bein' awful damn modest, Doc," he said. He walked up behind Crashnitz's chair and stood there with his arms crossed, a glass of bubbly clutched in a fist of fat fingers. Crashnitz knew he was there but kept staring straight ahead. "Guy here is the best in the business. You know what he overcame?"

Chip opened his eyes. He plumped his crotch with his fingers. He giggled.

"Not-me rejection," he said, like the punch line of an old comedy routine. He jammed his right foot against my dick for emphasis.

Crashnitz held up his hand, modest: "Plenty of pioneers in that area before I came along."

Mavis practically barked in protest: "Sure, other people figured out the immunosuppression aspects after a transplant procedure, but Guy here brought the mortality numbers *way* down." Mavis leaned forward and gazed into my face with what I guess you would call zeal. "See, Guy invented this chemical cocktail that completely fools your system so it can't tell what's you and what isn't you. Organ-wise. It's this molecular shield using two different antibodies, and Guy's the guy that came up with it."

When she'd get really animated, Mavis started to lisp a little: immunosuppression. I sat there nodding like an idiot, waving my glass and massaging Chip's toes, which was putting the little jerk into puppy heaven. I had like no idea what these people were talking about but it sounded, like, morbid. Next, Mavis wants to show me the set-up. So, feeling very floaty and out of control, I follow her out to the hall, through another sitting room with a door at the end that went downstairs.

You'd never imagine from outside the house, but the basement looks like a brand-new hospital. There's an examining room and a nurse's station and lots of little treatment rooms, plus what Mavis called "the kleine surgery," which has an operating table and all this equipment, radar, sonar, like I really know what, right? X-ray machines, lots of metal basins and bins and cabinets full of instruments and tools and what have you.

"We do a lot of our procedures right here, it really cuts down on hospital costs. You'd be surprised how a lot of so-called major surgery doesn't really require hospitalization."

I think they put something in my drink. I mean I only had one and I was getting this strange buzz of electric colors around the edges of things. My mind felt very scrambled. Like, why was this broad giving me the ten-cent tour through a fucking doctor's office, for one thing, and then, when we're back at the foot of the stairs, she makes a lunge for my bone, all the time whispering stuff I couldn't follow. Then she says, "Come on, Danny, fuck me quick, give me that fuck, they won't even know." What's even more bizarre, I get completely turned on, and before I like register what's happening her white nurse's skirt's up around her hips, no panties, and my cock is in her. Like I had on these button-fly Levis and she had the buttons open and the pants down around my knees so fast it was eerie. Mavis groans and whimpers like she's been starving for dick all day. "Ahhh, yeah, fuck it, fuck it, fuck that clam, Danny, that's good, that's good, that's right, uh, uh, oooh, that's a *big* prick, that's a *powerful* prick . . ." And I'm laughing the whole time I'm fucking her because everything she says breaks me up. Women who are verbal, man. It's rare. She has one of those pussies that just fucking gobbles you, that like supertight snatch that also at strategic moments throws open the floodgates and then clamps down hard on your meat when it's way inside, all the way in, all the way out, I fucking came in her which I really didn't plan on, and then we stood there shaking for about five minutes and fixed our clothes and went upstairs as if nothing had happened.

•

I've been laying low for a few days. Bruce is off on a sex holiday in Puerto Rico. I phoned in sick at the Emerson Club, in reality I wasn't feeling great and I need to be quiet for a while and like take care of the little things. For instance I bought some new dinner plates at Conran's and a better-designed bedside lamp than what I had. I also bought some books since I haven't read anything in months. It's hard to read. Things move too fast. I bought the complete poems of Elizabeth Bishop and a Dennis Cooper book Xavier told me about and just for laughs I bought the new Sandy Miller novel, *The Devil's Panties*, which has a quote from some minor cheese on the back that says reading Sandy Miller is like playing Scrabble with the Marquis de Sade, which I guess is a compliment, even though they didn't have Scrabble during the French Revolution.

My concentration is shot. This I realize. Yesterday Mavis was here. She just showed up. She got my address from Chip. It was weird. Instead of her nurse outfit she had on this green leatherette coat with a skanky fur collar and under that this tight beige dress. She said she was just passing by and thought I might feel like smoking a joint. Okay, fine. I make her a cup of tea and we do the joint which is very harsh and has some hash in it, and chitchat on this that and the other. She's trying to get some shopping done. At the clinic they work late practically every night and sometimes on weekends, too, it's exhausting work, she says, but rewarding, she thinks of herself and Guy and even Stanley as a team, helping people. I thought Stanley was just the butler or something but evidently he's more than that, though Mavis didn't give an exact job title. She's got her legs crossed and keeps uncrossing them and crossing them again and, I have to admit, I'm thinking the whole time about that oyster of hers, go figure. It probably sounds silly, she says, since half the time what we're really doing is collecting urine samples, but there's also the surgical side, and there you really get inside people and see what makes them tick. Mavis says this with a straight face but she obviously means it humorously, so I laugh, then she says, Well, it is funny, but on the other hand, why do you think people get into internal medicine anyway? They get off on opening people up, she says, it's what they enjoy.

Tell you the truth, I'm a little squeamish as far as the insides of other human beings are concerned, and I'm like real squeamish about my own insides, which so far, knock wood, haven't given me too many problems. I guess it's better to know what goes on in there, but let's face it, all that stuff inside you turns against you sooner or later and thinking about it day in day out could drive somebody right over the edge. I mean unless you're like Mavis or Doctor Crashnitz or whatever. Mavis drank her tea and I guess I took it for granted she wanted like an instant replay of our happiness on the stairs, I was kind of bracing myself for it, but instead she said, Has Guy spoken to you yet about a job?

Gee no, I says, I knew he had something in mind for Chip but I already have a job. Two jobs, in fact. So I tell her about Bruce and the Emerson Club, etcetera. She lights a Camel filter. I guess that's interesting, she says. I mean, you must come in contact with a lot of people. Well, I thought, that's the understatement of the year, but, yeah, definitely. How's the money, she says. Oh, I says, added to my, you know, outcall stuff, it adds up. She kind of scuffs the carpet with her shoes and clears her throat. The thing is, she says, Guy needs a couple guys to work on a special project of his, and whoever those guys are, they stand to acquire a nice little nest egg. But I guess he would've mentioned it if he had you in mind. I thought he said something about it, but maybe I heard him wrong.

I suddenly had this feeling that Mavis hadn't just dropped over. Nothing I could pin down, but I got the distinct impression that she was here to deliver a pitch. What do I know? I'm curious, who wouldn't be.

Well, I said, what's he got in mind?

It takes Mavis a really long time to get to the punchline so I'm going to shorten this but I'm like counting on you, J., to keep all this to yourself. Otherwise you could really get people in a lot of trouble and that wouldn't be especially healthy for you, either, a word to the wise. Okay, it's like this. In the urology department at the hospital they've got thousands of medical records on file, and they're understaffed because of budget cuts. Among other things Mavis does some filing where they keep the files for like six different specialists, and one time when they had a really pressing case of renal failure and were like making a public appeal for a kidney donor they combed through a lot of files of live patients with both kidneys in mint condition and actually called these people, though of course every one of them said no, even when Crashnitz made like an unofficial cash offer on behalf of the transplant patient.

That in itself was pretty illegal because they went into other doctors' medical records without permission. Nobody complained to the hospital and then the whole thing got resolved when some stiff's kidney became available. Most of the time they get the kidney off a stiff who's like signed a paper that his organs should go to science, only a lot of the time the organs aren't compatible or they're fresh out of kidneys, lungs, livers, hearts, eyeballs, whatever else they can use. It's a big problem.

In reality, Mavis said, a lot of stuff goes on at the big hospitals that isn't a hundred percent kosher. For instance, organs get shipped through these hospitals in like Third World countries, Egypt and so on, which have been donated by like starving families, they're willing to part with a kidney for a few thousand dollars, and by this time it's a regular industry, people selling parts of their own bodies for food money, and if you're a doctor in this country, you might have like a "special relationship" with these overseas hospitals where basically you become an organ importer, the stuff comes to you in these sterile containers and then you can sell it at an unbelievable markup. I mean there's no fixed price for a kidney, if somebody's gonna croak without getting one they'll pay just about anything.

So, in other words, certain hospitals aren't too picky about where they get the stuff as long as it's still palpitating or whatever. And after they went snooping through these patient records the first time, Mavis and Crashnitz got this . . . idea. As Mavis expressed it, they were pissed off at the selfishness of these people who like wouldn't even *sell* an organ they could perfectly well live without and would never miss, she said it seemed completely immoral, like those people who just ignore the homeless and walk past with all this spare change rattling in their pockets, money they'd otherwise use on a parking meter or leave it in their clothes for years at a time. And you can't legally do anything, Mavis said, you can't force somebody to donate, even if they're the one person in the world who could like save another human life.

But, she said, what if they themselves had an eenie weenie accident? Nothing serious, just a little brush with Mr. D. to teach them a lesson, and in the process perform a humanitarian service? Would that be wrong, to make that happen? I tried to visualize what she was talking about, she'd started lisping a little, the thing is, she says, *right at this very moment* there are, like, several critical cases, the patients are being managed on dialysis for the moment, and the organ bank has zero deposits in it, they've studied the whole thing very carefully and drawn up a list of ideal donors from other people's files. Stanley's been checking these people out. Stanley used to be a police detective, Mavis tells me. He knows where the people work, where they live, what their habits are. We even have taps on some of their telephones, Mavis says.

Call me retarded, but I'm still not getting it. Okay, you know where they live and what they do and all that, but what're you gonna do? Get some dirt on them and like *blackmail* them into donating their kidneys?

By this time Mavis was stoned and started laughing. She's kind of stunning when she laughs but a little scary, too. Like I said before, Mavis is a goodtime gal, very what you'd call *giving.* But underneath it there's something hard and basically indifferent to people and it shows in her face.

She's thinking all the time, Mavis. And what she's thinking is, What's in it for me? Believe me, you do what I do for a living you recognize that look a mile off. Which I'm not condemning or anything, it takes one to know one.

Not a bad idea, she howls. I can just see that, phone up some businessman at home, tell him, Your wife's gonna find out you were eating some guy's asshole in the Port Authority restroom if you don't give us one of your internal organs. You know? There's probably plenty of guys who would do it!

Well, it struck me funny, too, and we kind of choked up and cried on our own laughter for a few minutes and then she kept laughing and I stopped laughing and I felt these frozen fingers moving up my spinal cord and I looked at Mavis's legs and Mavis's pink fingernail polish and I said: Let's cut to the chase, Mavis, what's the fucking scam.

It's three-thirty in the morning. I know you're sitting in your apartment reading this and I said I'd tell you everything that happens to me and I will, but I'm like too wiped out to go on right now. I'll stick this in the mail and write down the rest of it after I hear from you again because you owe me two letters. I miss seeing you. I also think you're a real cunt. You said we'd try this for a while and then we could get together again and it's what, three months now? Four months? You want me to say the magic words? You think they mean anything?

Okay, you guessed right. It's this shanghai operation they've been planning, the three of them, for a long time now. The mark's name is a Mr. Lindner, who lives up in

Westchester County but runs some genetic engineering consortium and likes to kick back at the end of the day in La Esqualita and Sally's II, drag places in the Forties. He had a little heart problem a few years ago so he can't drink liquor. Smokes a little dope and has been known to pick up "girls" that he takes to the less elegant hotels in the area. He's married, natch, with kids, but he's got a real yen for pre-ops. He absolutely does not like "men," so we figured it was cool for Chip and me to check him out one night without getting noticed.

Stanley has been trailing this guy for weeks, so he came with us into La Esqualita, which was packed, since they were just starting the floorshow. The floorshow sucked. Big drags in sequins doing bad lip-sync, but the place looked full of straight people anyway who go ape over any type of drag number because to them it's like real "transgressive." That's a word Sandy Miller kind of infects people with. Anyway, our mark was all by himself at the bar, where it wasn't too crowded, trying to make himself interesting to a Spanish kid with a long black wig and a feather boa and the kind of dress Jackie Kennedy had on in that motorcade. The kid looked glazy bored under all the eye makeup and Lindner, all dolled up in his office suit, wasn't trying *too* hard. Actually, he's not a bad-looking guy, kind of like John Cassavetes in *Rosemary's Baby* but a little older and the hair more or less totally gray.

Stanley left us there once we had him spotted. The guy looked pretty quick on his feet, and like I said, he can't drink, so there's no chance of getting him shit-face drunk. Anyway, we just wanted to make sure we'd be able to recognize him again. I drank a beer. Chip ordered a brandy and soda and drank two of them down, quick, and I could see he was nervous, just thinking about what we were doing there and what it was leading up to, even though this was only a reconnaissance flight so to speak. I mean I had the thought that we'd already gotten into this to the point of no turning back. It's true I haven't given them a yes or a no, but in a way just letting Mavis tell me the whole scam was the same thing as saying yes. Wasn't it? Because, okay, I'm thinking the whole time about Chip, how he's incredibly careless about shit and could really fuck the thing up on his own, or like in league with one of his churns from Trix, Fat Paul the moron or what have you, ending up in the federal slammer or wherever they put you for kidnapping.

I think you know me well enough to know I don't buy Mavis's crap about doing this shit for the good of humanity. Obviously we're all doing this for money. Fifteen grand for Chip, fifteen for me, and Christ knows what untold thousands for Guy Crashnitz and his cronies. Fifteen plus the ten I've got salted away from hustling would buy a lot of peace and quiet, even in the city. I don't have extravagant needs. My rent's, you know, reasonable. But what I'm thinking, see, sublet the apartment and go down to Mexico for a while. You can live for a *long* time on $25,000 in Mexico. I'm aware of the fact that this is big-time criminal shit, but tell you frankly, it's small time compared with what some of these CEO types you run across in Rounds get away with every day of their lives.

We haven't set the date. I get the feeling that it's pretty soon. I've been back to that house a few times, it's always the same deal: champagne, some incredible dinner from the caterer, Mavis like regaling everybody with her stories. Now that we're all like engaged in criminal activity together there's this weird kind of speedy excitement in the air. Chip's really punch-drunk on the whole thing, and if you ask me, doing a lot of smack. He talks to you like there's forty layers of cotton batting between his mouth and his brain, but it all comes out real elegant and slow and he's got this big panoramic look in his eyes. Crashnitz's practically jolly, lurches out of his wing chair to pour champagne, stumps around the room with his walking-stick tossing off witty remarks, offers these fat lines of coke, chops it up with a razor blade himself. "So one time, in the service, I'm performing an emergency gastrojejunostomy on an enlisted man whose guts were all plugged up with shrapnel . . . there we were, a hundred yards from the battlefield . . . this was Korea, young man, stupidest war this country ever fought. I was a medic like in *M*A*S*H*. But believe me, it wasn't fun and games. No big-tit nurses or orderlies in drag clothes. Just the dull bloody business of death in the ugliest manner possible. They bring this poor kid named Dave to the surgery tent with half his guts dangling out and some junkie had purloined my morphine. Anyway . . ." Stanley, too, all wired up, he's got his cop stories, his glory days as a detective—on vice, absolutely perfect. He used to entrap people in the toilets at Bloomingdale's.

But the real bon vivant has got to be Mavis. Before she became an RN, Mavis danced topless at the Baby Doll Lounge and some other venues in the business district. She also dealt, you know, coke and shit, MDA, small-time smack, reefer, Quaaludes, you name it, out of her place in the West Village, mostly to big wheels in the entertainment industry. Quite a resume. I don't think we're going to fuck again. The vibration has been like eclipsed by this new energy. Fucking on the stairs was more like her way of saying hello. Even Chip got it up for her, and he's one person with absolutely no use for pussy most of the time. Of course in our business you have to stay versatile but there really aren't any women clients. That only happens in the movies. Yesterday I did Charlie, a monthly client, lives in a spacious two-bedroom, slightly rundown place with lots of mementos and movie-star fan photos framed on the walls, real obscure ones like of Judy Canova and Maria Ouspenskaya and George Macready. There's one of Gene Tierney and Victor Mature in *Shanghai Gesture*, one of the nuttiest movies I've ever seen, Rita Hayworth as a blonde in *The Lady From Shanghai*, he's also got Roman Polanski in drag from *The Tenant*, a signed one of Candy Darling, etcetera. You would think he'd be a big queen, but he's pretty much a regular guy, if a little depraved. There's also a bunch of war photographs, not war in the sense of blood and explosions, I mean cabinet photos of Marshal Pétain and Mussolini and that type of charismatic personality, Franco, Hitler natch, Eva Péron, Stalin, these movie stars from old newsreels that people never get tired of. Pol Pot. You know. Charlie's what, maybe forty, a Jew, his hair's going back, slightly dumpy, got an accordion roll on his waist anyway, a little beard of hair on his sternum, pudgy hairy legs, he's going to a gym but tells me it's a losing battle, he likes Ben & Jerry's too much, and his little pleasures . . . he's an author, I actually met him at the Emerson Club, or rather I waited on him, and then by coincidence he called my ad in *The Advocate* one night . . . that was during my "Ten Hard Inches of Heaven" ad . . . very sweet voice . . . writes celebrity bios and shit . . . nice guy, pretty straightforward . . . he always gives me a shot of scotch beforehand, or a little Rémy, not that I generally drink brown liquor, it gives me a mean headache.

Anyway, he's pretty comical . . . loves getting boned, a real acrobat . . . one leg over my shoulder, the other one thrown out . . . then both Achilles tendons on the same shoulder, tossing his ass to one side . . . flips around to take it from behind . . . sits on it facing away from me, squishing up and down and watching the action in a mirror . . . "God, I look ridiculous," he says . . . all the time snorting from a popper bottle . . . eases himself off my prong, gets me kneeling on top of him . . . peels off the condom and starts sucking the old love tub, slathers my balls . . . next he's maneuvered his head under there and works his tongue up into my asshole . . . feels great . . . slurping away like a deer with a salt lick . . . then slides another condom on me with his mouth, real professional, I don't even feel it going on . . . squats over . . . I'm pronging him with my torso arched back, now I'm looking in the mirror, his face's squashed into a pillow . . . I slap his ass so hard my fingers leave blood-red imprints . . . he churns his hole like a chorus girl doing the can-can . . . suddenly I feel a kind of extra squish . . . a strange resistance . . . well, not so strange . . . his hole's getting plugged up, I realize that I'm, you know, squishing shit, like my prick has burst through some toll booth on the Hershey Highway where all the extra shit's in storage, I look down and see it, all beige and cakey, stuck to the condom, and smeared on the part of my dick where there's like two inches the condom doesn't cover. What the hell, I keep fucking . . . only know it's a mechanical type thing, I can't really get my mind off that globbed-up feces for some reason . . . it doesn't stink or anything but there's lots of it, a real thick coating . . . two-toned . . . maple walnut and dark Swiss chocolate . . . I think, what if he's infected and some of that slithers down inside the condom and leaks into my urethra or whatever . . . knowing, you know, that it's practically impossible . . . for one thing the rubber's so tight it's cutting off my circulation . . . my cock looks like a blood sausage bursting from its casing . . . but once that thought slips in, I flash on all the extra-dubious sexcapades I've been involved in, all the little slip-ups, for instance there's one dude, and I don't think he ever plans this or anything, but sometimes, we'll get into action, and the rubber just doesn't feel right against his orifice, he'll try it one way then another way and then, five or six times now, we kind of silently disengage and roll the thing off and diddle around for a while pretending we're going to slip on another one, he's just gonna smooth a little ForePlay over my bone for a minute and keep me excited, then he starts rubbing his ass lips against the head of my john henry with a corkscrew motion, not enough at first to draw it in but after a few seconds we both know it's gonna happen . . . the first time, I really only pushed it halfway in, for like ten seconds or something, and then we froze kind of horrified and wiped off the lubricant and put a Trojan on it, but the next time we did a date the barrier was already down, we're both thinking, "Well, we've already done this with each other, and he probably does it safe with everybody else, so if he's exposed or I'm exposed we exposed each other that last time, and if we're not exposed, we're not gonna be," at least that's what I was thinking, but really not believing it.

The bitch of it is, it's a zillion times more swishy without the fucking condom, it's like you feel the other person's insides all warm and wet, you really feel yourself inside them, it's two people losing themselves in each other's bodies, except of course the whole time I'm also thinking, "This has death in it, this is life and it's also death." Which makes it into this amazing intricate act like skydiving with a parachute that maybe isn't going to open, only you won't know if it did or not for five or ten years. And the fisting, with this or that customer, more like fingering but what's the difference, I've always got these tiny paper cuts and nicks on my fingers and people have every type of body fluid up in their rectums, you just never fucking know.

Charlie like apologized profusely for the crap, he said he douched for a half an hour before I came over. I kept telling him it was nothing, it is nothing, lots of times you get a little crap on your dick, but when I left his place, which is up in Chelsea, it hit me for the first time ever: I thought, Jesus, I am really tired of this scene. I felt like my brain was full of novocaine, and I walked down Lexington kind of aimless, past all those Indian restaurants and the Armory, and I ended up, you know, in the cocktail bar at the Gramercy, first I bought the *Times* at the newsstand and then I had a Coke in the bar. It's funny how sex passes right through you, I was already forgetting all about the date I just had, and then I decided to stroll around the park. It really is spring now, finally.

You can see Crashnitz's house from one corner of the park, and up the street there's the clinic entrance, which looks like a separate building because there's a kind of concrete add-on behind the house with a sloped garage entrance . . . not real conspicuous, it's kind of angled back behind the houses on the next street . . . there was a white stretch limousine double-parked in front of the garage, pointed up Twenty-First Street. Kids were pouring out of Washington Irving High in little navy and white school uniforms, colored girls in pigtails, boys in baseball caps lighting up reefers . . . it's crazy, you know, you walk by any bunch of male kids, they could be seven years old, and chances are one of them's calling another one a faggot . . . so these fucked-up attitudes just get passed on from one generation to the next one . . . the light at that time of day through the trees reminded me, I don't know, a little bit of Italy, the time I was in Italy . . . the Tuscany hills. Most of the shutters were closed on the upper windows of Crashnitz's place. I figured Chip would be just staggering out of bed up there, luxuriating . . . I thought, maybe he'd like to see a movie, eat something . . . but I had to think about it, too, because it gives me the creeps going into that place, I can't help it . . . especially now . . . so I'm standing at the edge of the park, smoking a joint, just like the school kids . . . and this guy saunters out of the clinic . . . right away the chauffeur leaps out of the limo and scurries around to open the back door . . . big guy with a puffy face and bulging eyes, very tailored, long beige cashmere coat . . . he gets in the car real fast, but right away I recognized him, how could you help it, it's that developer billionaire Stagpole they've always got plastered all over the tabloids . . . I think I told you I waited on him once, anyway I would've known him from his pictures. Then the limo glides away up Twenty-First toward Park Avenue . . . the windows are all one-way glass, like panels of onyx . . . I guess his kidneys are acting up . . .

I came home, I canceled a date I had for later that night, this soap opera actor over at the Chelsea Hotel who digs eating turds . . . like he has you go, right, and then fishes it out of the bowl and leaves it on a plate for a half hour "in case of the virus," he says. According to him, HIV can't survive outside the body more than ten minutes. Never mind all the other wiggy viruses and microbes that stick around in your ca-ca until it dissolves somewhere, but I mean, it's his funeral. Scat is another thing I thought was really freaky the first time, watching this Siegfried blonde out of a *GQ* spread chowing down one of my bowel movements, not real demurely, either . . . like a kid with a chocolate bar, smacking it all over his mouth . . . everything else about Morgan is completely normal, dig, he's got *The Magic Flute* enchanting us on his CD player, scented candles throwing a soft romantic glow against the walls . . . gobbles it up with his fingers, sometimes sips a piquant but oakey chablis with it . . . and if he's really in a baroque mood, he watches me do things, stroke myself or finger my asshole or pull on my nipples or whatever, but usually he keeps all his clothes on, dress clothes like it's a formal sit-down dinner . . . maybe pulls his dong out of his pants and whacks himself off with shit all over his fingers . . . it's bizarre how easy it is, getting used to scenes like that, once you know what the client wants and it's all established you just walk through it like an old dressing room. I had enough shit for one day, though. I'm never worried about canceling on a regular client or anybody else for that matter, they might get pissed off and like pout over the telephone but in the end, you know, who else is he gonna get to come over and watch him eat shit? Not too many people you'd trust in a hotel room. Probably nobody from his soap opera gig, either.

A lot of clients don't open up with their peculiarities on the first date. Sometimes you don't find out for months what they're really into. You might only get little hints while doing regular sex. Then they can introduce it as a novelty item, like they just thought of something wild to spice things up. Because they're a little embarrassed. Maybe they think it's sick if they enjoy licking assholes or having guys piss on them *more* than they dig sucking or getting fucked, but to me, the offbeat scenes break up the monotony. It's intriguing, what I can say? Especially when they've got a wiggy obsession I never heard of, that I'd never even think I could get off on. They get so excited, once they see I'm not, like, judgmental about it, and really encourage them to have a good time, it completely turns me on. Stuff that doesn't necessarily require an erection takes the pressure off. Which somehow makes it easier to *get* an erection, you know?

Yesterday I thought I was coming down sick: stomach shit, like I'd puke if something untoward happened, which made it kind of iffy to check in with Bruce. He claimed he had an emergency, so right away I thought, I'll get over there and he'll tell me he's got AIDS, but all it was, he had to photograph a salad for a ladies' magazine, avocado with pear slices, and there was nobody else around in the studio for some reason, so he sends me down to Dean & DeLuca for the produce and it's like a dollar fifty for a fucking avocado, plus all these jumped-up horror couples and their brats squashed into strollers, grazing around in Agnes B. jumpers and spring wear from Barney's, lining up to pay a million dollars for a half a pound of designer raviolis or a cheese sandwich. You know, they've got a special guy to plastic wrap and price your vegetables, you can't just take them to the checkout, it's like this church where everybody worships overpriced food.

I'm in line there, you know, with Bruce's credit card, and I get this wave of nausea, not enough to heave or anything but all the objects on the wooden takeout counter are suddenly standing out in like garish relief, the pebbled lizard skin of the avocados, the little blackhead specks on the yellow pears, and those tartan display boxes of Scottish shortbread cakes or what have you, I felt this bizarre clammy sweat breaking out on my chest and my stomach, and this tall athletic broad in front of me has a wire basket full of every possible and impossible snob food items, mostly packaged in white paper, what can I tell you, this woman, who's dressed up for tennis and looks like a real estate ad for Sagaponick beachfront, gives me a look, she's just unsnapping the Chanel pocketbook and fishing for the credit card, she pauses like a movie freeze frame and our eyes locked and in that moment I felt completely exposed, as if all my stupid desires were hanging out of my pants or I had a sign around my neck Cock For Sale. I'm not saying this the right way, it wasn't anything to do with shame or embarrassment but just this awful nausea becoming the total focus of my consciousness, like my whole life and everything in it had converged on one moment of time and one overpowering knot in my stomach. And all these objects around me, lumps of food and people in their clothes and eyewear and everything, filling up space until I couldn't breathe, and I thought if I just put my hand on the checkout counter it would burn a hole in the wood, or pass through it like a hologram. I felt . . . unbelievably tired. Tired to the point where I could no longer protect myself from reality, if that makes any sense.

So we shot this garden salad and Bruce brings out his deluxe Russian egg full of coke, spooning it up his nostrils and jabbering God knows what about some party he went to at the Royalton, Bianca this Bianca that and Calvin and Kelly and blah blah blah, I said I didn't want any coke which seemed to put him off but he kept on talking, we sat on his green leather sofa smoking cigarettes, I knew if I did one whiff of cocaine I'd throw up immediately, and Bruce puts his hand on my pants, something he does a whole lot—I'm wearing those patchwork ruffled jeans, so there's all this tacky fringe for him to play with—yacking and yacking like I'm not gonna notice his palm rubbing up and down my thigh, he keeps giving me these shady glances, checking to see if I'm getting a boner. I was a little hard, it's true. Bruce can be kind of an exciting guy because he's so out there about being horny all the time, and the way he disrespects his work, not his work per se but the subject matter, all this food, when you work with him you always feel you're breaking all these rules of fashion or propriety or something, and of course he's not bad looking either, he's got that pretty WASP thing going and the memory traces of a gym bod, he used to keep it up, if he got his nose bobbed he'd look like one of Bruce Weber's wet dreams on a bad day, and he's all bitched up for some reason in a burnt orange Thierry Mugler number, like a Dean & DeLuca carrot.

"So, Billy," he says, dropping his hand on my crotch. (I use the name Billy with Bruce.) "Now we've got Family Circle out of the way I thought we could have a little private moment together."

I thought about that.

"That would be cool, Bruce," I said, "if it wasn't for the fact I'm really sick."

"What do you mean sick?" Just that word, you know, and the shadow of AIDS flaps across his gray eyes, his hand flutters off my basket like a frightened parakeet. "What's the trouble?" Bruce makes this *really concerned* face.

"I've been sick to my stomach all day," I said, rubbing it and like wincing. "I picked up a bug somewhere."

He gives that a little thought and recovers his helpful nurse smile. Then, real sincere: "Sometimes, Billy, I'd really like to shoot some pictures of you. I don't know why you're not in modeling. You'd be perfect for it."

Bruce doesn't realize, everybody knows this is his signature tune. I act real flattered and, you know, fucked up about my looks: "Jeez, Bruce, some of- those guys are really gorgeous. I mean"—I give him a self-deprecating smirk—"I've got a real average face in comparison."

He leaps off the sofa, literally, and spins around, throwing his arms out, energizing the moment with a freak show of coke gestures.

"You putting me on, Billy? You're fuckin' *beautiful*, man, as if you didn't know. You should hear the assistants whenever your name comes up. Where'd you *find* him, Bruce? What's his phone number, I wanna give him a *call*."

I'm actually surprised that Bruce never ran across my phone number in *The Advocate*, it's the same one he's got in his Rolodex and I know he goes over the Escort and Massage pages with a yellow marker for reference.

"We could do *nudes*, we could do *headshots*, send you up to *Click*, fix you up with *Martin* up at *Zoli* . . . I'd make the *referral*, Billy."

He drops down on the couch again, he's so excited he shovels three spoons up his nose and rocks back and forth as if his brain's spinning too fast for him to keep up with it.

"*I* just wish you weren't sick," he says, "for my own selfish reasons—don't mind me saying so, Billy, the day you walked in that door with that big sexy grin of yours I thought, I sure wouldn't mind getting it on with that one. I mean, we fool around up here but I normally don't get too involved with an employee."

"Well," I say, like this is also my biggest regret, "any time but now, Bruce, I'm game—"

"It's your stomach's fucked up? Would it . . . make it worse if I . . . uh . . . oh, I dunno, rubbed your dick for a little while?"

Bruce turns real soft and romantic which isn't like him at all, and a little scary, like most hard people when they're being nice. Like I can see he's been thinking about this for a long time and just decided today was the day, hop on that bone, fuck what condition *I'm* in: that's why he's alone in the studio. Bruce is one of those rich queens who's always had a house on Fire Island and a bevy of mannequins and jewelry designers dropping in for Sunday brunch, that type of disco queen shading into clone and in Bruce's case into heavy M who like lives in an all-queer world more or less, at that moment I could see him brimming over with these artificial emotions that would dissolve without a trace as soon as he'd had what he wanted. It's kind of an old-fashioned way for queers to relate to each other but Bruce never gave up the '70s, somehow.

I figured I had to be diplomatic, he's such a drama queen. I even thought about pulling it out and letting him chow down so I wouldn't have to keep talking to him, but then the nausea kicked in and I had to fly for the toilet and brought up everything I'd eaten all day, probably shit from the day before too, pink muck that stank like a sidewalk in August with stuff that looked like twigs and nuts chunked into it, I'm wondering, what the fuck *did* I eat, and Bruce's standing over me making sympathetic noises but also calculating I'm not any use to him in this condition, he's got a cocktail party at five, he's wondering who he could beep for a fast bang. I got out of there but first we had to make a bunch of wounded bird noises at each other like we'd had this wonderful talk and become much closer than we'd been before. I acted like I'd seen Bruce's vulnerable human side for the first time and come to realize what a truly majestic guy he really was, and he had this "Don't thank me, that's just the way I am" thing on his face.

At least I felt better having puked. I thought I'd go crash out at home and recover, maybe read the Dennis Cooper book I bought a few weeks ago, but in the cab I changed my mind and told the driver to zip up to Forty-Second and Eighth Avenue. We were already on Third heading into Chelsea so he turns up Twenty-First, it's just starting rush hour and the streets are clogged and the cab crawls past Crashnitz's place, I'm thinking I'll see Chip or maybe Mavis coming out of there, but the house looks dead, and that big limo's double-parked again near the clinic entrance. Stagpole's limo. The driver's like invisible behind the black glass, and I try to remember what the driver looked like the last time, but the traffic picked up, and what can I tell you, I shivered going past that place and felt glad to get away from there. You know, the thing is all set, it's just a question of the date.

So I run into Bobby Larkin at the Port Authority, Bobby used to be the regular boyfriend of that priest at Covenant House, one of these misguided youths with a big prong Father Candyass set up in a studio love nest for a few years before they blew the whistle on him. Bobby's at FIT in his second year now and his pork is still very much in demand in that neighborhood, thanks to Chelsea Gym and a distant resemblance to Rob Lowe. His lawsuit against Father Candyass has been dragging on a long time, if he wins he's off the game for good but while he's on the game he's got to be, like, a little bit discreet in case of detectives who will then go into court and say what a big strumpet he still is since Father Candyass's lawyers claim that Bobby's quote unquote incorrigible and always was and like lured Candyass down the primrose path in spite of being a juvenile.

I bought a small bottle of Pepto-Bismol in one of the shops and drank the whole thing on the escalators. We went up to the top level into that bar at the bowling alley. It's a nice place for a beer, roll a few balls. We sat inside the bar and watched the bowling through the windows, meanwhile they've got a game on TV, basketball, which Bobby is up on though I couldn't care less, Chicago Bulls, you can have them, I'm sipping my soda water and Bobby chugs down three Dos Equis while pounding the counter urging on Michael Jordan along with the bartender and all these half-soused suits at the bar, and through the window I can see this guy Juan and this other guy Freddy from the Latino Fan Club bowling like really badly, throwing gutter balls and breaking each other up like they're high, vogueing for whatever customers the bowling alley has to offer. I was actually feeling better. Almost good enough to turn a trick.

"We could check out Hombre."

"Place stinks like fucked cunt, forget it."

"Or the toilets, do a commuter . . ."

"You look like you're nervous, Danny."

"Think I'm coming down with something."

"You should get out of town for a while. Los Angeles."

"I hate L.A."

"Yeah, but you could do some videos. You ever do videos?"

"I don't know if it's a cold or the flu or what."

"They like my all-American boy-next-door type in that L.A. stuff."

"I mean, it's run, run, run, all day every day."

"Here, lately, they just wanna see spic and nigger bone, go figure."

"My immune system's probably shot to hell."

"Not that I got anything against, you know? Hell, I'm hung like a nigger, I probably got a touch of the tarbrush somewhere anyway. You think your immune system's shot, mine's fucking pickled."

"You haven't seen Chip around, have you?"

"Shit, man, I did, you know, maybe a week ago. At La Fleur. Funny you mention him, I'll tell you, because he was out with this heavy fucking snatch—"

"Ratty hair? Bleach blond?"

"Yeah, yeah, acres of blue eye shadow, but get this, Danny, I *know* this bitch, at least I think it's the same one, I'm all fucked up in Hombre one night and she's like perched on a bar stool next to me, for about ten minutes I thought she was a drag queen, and then she strikes up this really friendly conversation, this is like a week before I saw her with Chip, she's like coming on to me about how she can get really pure dope, would I be interested, and you know, Danny, if I could kick I fucking would, man, but I never did lose a taste for skag, people just don't.

"Anyway, she says she's got a room in the Edison, and some speedballs, I'd be welcome to, like, come up and get to know her better. See, I thought it was about sex, so I laid it out, I said I don't perform too hot with women, then she said she didn't care about that, anyway she's got a pussy infection, she just wanted some company. So, we go up there, it's one of the better rooms, and she takes out works, she takes out dope, she cleans the needle with bleach and so forth, very safe, and we get royally fucked up, you could've peeled me off the ceiling. And because of the speed we're rapping, you know, and she asks all these questions like my existence really fascinates her, the whole trip with Father Cornhole and my lawsuit etcetera, and it gets on to money, as in, what type of things you would do, for how much money and so forth.

"Oh, yeah, and she's got the TV on the Home Shopping Club, they're showing you marquise diamonds, they're showing you Chanthaburi emeralds, and that dyke that looks like Joan Rivers is describing how you're not gonna find this cocktail ring in a setting of white gold anywhere else for less than fifteen hundred dollars, the gold setting alone is making her pussy damp, and this babe—the real one, I mean—asks me if I'd, you know, do somebody for like five grand."

"Do meaning fuck? Who'd she have in mind, Cardinal O'Connor?"

"Get with the program, Danny, do meaning homicide. Says she's got a friend who's probably gonna find himself with a major disposal problem on his hands about a month from now. Two disposal problems, if you wanna get technical, but one's like a part-time addict that would only need a hot shot, the other one could go out the same way but might need to be, how did she put it, restrained."

All of a sudden my stomach acids kind of ate through the Pepto-Bismol.

"She mention anything about who it was?"

"Well, I told her I wasn't interested before I got too many details. She said it would probably be a couple of rent boys and maybe I'd know them and that would make getting the job done a whole lot easier. I should've gotten more pissed off than I did, now I think about it. Just because a person did a little time doesn't mean they're up for like chilling their associates, right?"

I dropped out of Rutgers or dropped a semester or whatever because I'm sick of driving out there. I hardly ever take the car out of the parking lot on Twenty-Sixth Street because this city is so torn up and full of potholes and collapsed areas and repair crews you might as well be in Cambodia, besides which I am finding it kind of ludicrous to keep my mind on French Gardens. Last night at the Emerson Club we had Lauren Hutton and Malcolm McLaren at a table with that tub-of-lard painter that did the broken plates years ago, fatso had about four complete entrees while the others just picked at their food. Whatever they didn't finish, Dumbo the Elephant speared with his fork and gobbled it up. I'm surprised he's not fatter than he is but I guess he burns it off splashing paint around and yacking about himself from the time he wakes up till the time all that food lays him out. David Humphreys, natch, sashayed around their table all night like Diotima, bought them a bottle of Veuve Clicquot and a bunch of Rémys, though I noticed Lauren Hutton was drinking plain Pellegrino and planting her own beverages in front of fatso. Lauren Hutton is really beautiful and you can tell she's a nice woman, too. 1 was shaky all night and when Sandy Miller waltzed in, all in motorcycle gear and eleven earrings in her nostrils, I figured we were in for an evening of real glitz and glam, she had a bunch of Brits trailing after her who took the big center table. She said she just signed her contract for that bodybuilding book and she had this author Edna something with her and the rest were all these leering fifty-something boozers in town for the ABA. Anyway, Sandy cornered me on her way to the gents', which she always uses on principle, and says: "You know something, Mark, you really look like shit tonight, is something wrong?"

Since Sandy never notices anything about anybody, I figured I should maybe use the gents' myself and check the mirror. My face was dead white, and I mean dead. And I suddenly realized my whole body below the collar was sweating. Not, you know, copious, but the Emerson Club is air-conditioned. Next thing I'm in the pay phone calling Chip but Stanley answers the phone and says he's not there and furthermore where the fuck have I been, they're gonna move on the item like very, very pronto, and there's been some adjustments he can't go into on the telephone I need to be informed about. So I said I'd come the next day but Stanley says Wait a second and puts Mavis on the line.

Hi hon, she says all chipper, you kind of disappeared on us there, everything's ready. There's a few last-minute details, we should just run through them tonight.

So I tell her I'm on my shift until one, I've got this real apprehension snaking up my back and figure one a.m. will put them off, but Mavis says anytime after one is just fine, they're planning what she calls some surprise festivities "because it's been a little gloomy around here, waiting for the big night. The scenario just needs another little touch or two," she says. Well, I've glommed a couple of little touches up at the bowling alley that Mavis isn't planning to tell us about, but the main thing, this is what I'm thinking, is to get Chip out of there and like blow the whistle on the whole deal. Except who the fuck's going to listen to a couple of male hookers anyway. The best thing would be for Chip to just, you know, vanish from Gramercy Park, but I've got no idea where he is or even if he'd believe the stuff Bobby Larkin told me. And another thought crossed my mind, chalk it up to paranoia, but what if like the plans have altered a little, let's say Mavis and Chip've become big-time horse buddies, and the idea is for me to get wasted instead of both of us? Like, maybe they want Chip to stay on as a permanent organ collector and he's buying the idea—he's always got some halfwit notion of how to get off the game, who knows, with enough dope melting his brainpan maybe the segue from trainee paramedic to kidnapper-hit man wouldn't strike him as a completely losing proposition.

My nerves are shot to shit. I copped a ten-milligram valium from Xavier in the changing room and then spotted a small KS lesion on his lower back just above the elastic of his underpants. At least it looked like one. What are you supposed to say? "Sure hope that isn't AIDS, dude." Then as I'm leaving the Emerson Club, Sandy Miller's out front hopping on her Harley, I like wave, and she motions me over, she lifts the plastic visor of her helmet and asks if I need a ride anywhere. She's on her way to some dive that's a leather sex club and doesn't open until after four, she's killing some time—which is rare for Sandy, Sandy has every minute of her existence scheduled and occupied, I think she'd fly into ten million pieces if she didn't—so I tell her I'm going to Gramercy Park and she hands me the spare helmet and we tear off into the wilds of stinking old New York City at night, the valium's kicking in and I've got my arms around Sandy's waist and there's mist in the air, blue-white mist like the vanishing residue of scenes and people gone long ago, it made you feel there was still some magic in the world somewhere, and the way Sandy drove the bike in this firm and definite pattern, zooming right through the sorry details of the streets as if she was headed for better times, better places, better people—well, I understood that bike was the closest she could get to a feeling of freedom. I couldn't see her face but I knew she was happy, and for ten minutes so was I.

It's funny, but ever since I started with this Crashnitz and Mavis and Stanley shit, Sandy's writing makes a lot more sense to me. I mean I feel like a character in a Sandy Miller novel most of the time lately.

Crashnitz himself opened the door and eyed me with his head cocked at that peculiar angle made by the hunch in his back, as if he was trying to place me. He wore this strange black moiré type of robe that shimmered in wavy patterns when he moved. Then that voice of his, kind of a gravelly whine: "Why Danny boy, the pipes the pipes are caw-wa-ling . . ."

I have never seen a man who seemed more in control of himself and the universe than Guy Crashnitz with his spidery fingers crawling around on the head of his cane. They should've broke the mold *before* they made that one, if you ask me. Because the guy has power. The voice, the eyes, the face: he practically turns you into a zombie on the spot. We went into the big salon, and get this, Mavis is playing Gershwin on the grand piano, she's wearing this aubergine dress from some designer like Valentino, and she's got her hair styled, I mean all unratted and dyed black and cut like, who else, Louise Brooks in *Pandora's Box*, with that vivid '30s makeup that's more like a vamp than a slut, and on the piano lid, on top of this chocolate velvet shawl, are these fat black candles in little ornamental tubs, plus regular tapered candles all over the room, and because of the lighting I could finally make out the figure in the stained glass window from the lead outside. It's a Pre-Raphaelite thing of Judith with the bloody head of Holofernes, she's in a flowy white gown holding a sword in the other hand. Of course in the candlelight it all looked kind of dull and burnished and pretty in that faded Pre-Raphaelite way. But creepy.

So Crashnitz sits down in one of those leather sling chairs and crosses his legs and hunches forward with his liver-spotted hands on the cane, kind of swaying it back and forth to the piano, while Mavis does the "Rhapsody in Blue," which I think used to be Oscar Levant's signature tune on the Jack Paar Show, not that I was around then. Mavis's piano style is pretty grandiose for a registered nurse, but people are full of surprises. This gets even better, though. Because while she's playing that section that really evokes some picture-book New York penthouse skyline at night with Claudette Colbert in a brace of diamonds and a Vionnet evening gown, I hear these steps coming down from the second floor and sweeping along the hall, and into the candlelight comes this like vision of loveliness in a silk wedding dress and a bridal bonnet, carrying a bouquet of cape jasmine and baby's breath. I had just looked away from the stained glass window and flashed for a second on *Hush . . . Hush Sweet Charlotte*, that scene in the beginning where Bruce Dern's hand gets chopped off with a meat cleaver during the wedding festivities. The bride's face is ghostly white, except for real thick Italian lips painted in blood red, okay, she's got kind of a wide nose and mannish cheeks and large slightly hooded brown eyes, but she's totally ethereal and glides along into the room like an ectoplasm pushed by the breeze from a small desk fan. And Mavis is pounding the ivories, she jumps from Gershwin to "Non, Je Regrette Rien," and Crashnitz closes his eyes and nods to the music real emphatic with his chin, the bride floats along the carpet to the center of the salon and hovers right next to the Giacometti, lifting her arms above her head, swinging the bouquet and filling the room with the smell of jasmine. The music's crashing around us, at first I stood there like an idiot staring and finally I moved toward her, how can I put it, we were all together there in the room, with the candles flickering, and Judith holding the bloody head by a tangle of auburn curls, and Stanley walks into the room pushing an operating room gurney blazing with candles and this four-story wedding cake, plus a square mirror with a cone of cocaine ringed with single-edge razor blades, and at this point Mavis segues into one of those Erik Satie piano pieces that were so popular twenty years ago, a little bit somber and just a wee bit, you know, ominous, and then I pull Chip close to me and kiss him on the mouth and then my tongue is in his mouth and I can taste his lipstick, and his arms go around me with the bridal bouquet still clutched in one fist, I feel his boner against mine through the wedding dress, and behind me I hear Stanley chopping up lines of coke on the mirror, then wheeling the gurney over to Crashnitz who snorts about four lines, then the rubber wheels of the gurney creak across the carpet to Mavis, who breaks off playing and toots quite a large quantity of powder. The silence at that point was like those movies of A-bombs going off, that flash before there's any noise, and I'm grinding my crotch into Chip's, he's kissing me all over my face, and next it's our turn for the coke, in dead silence except for the wheels of the gurney and Stanley clearing his throat and Crashnitz snuffling up whatever's still in his nostrils.

Chip kind of backs away from me to snuffle up a fat worm of coke. Then he straightens up and says:

"Bobby Larkin's a fuckin' liar."

Well, J., I don't need to tell you, shades of evening fall and paranoia strikes deep, into your soul it will creep. I like hadn't said a word about Bobby Larkin and Mavis chimes right in behind him: "The fact is, we offered him this job and he agreed. We even let him stay here and what do you suppose, he stole about a thousand dollars' worth of silverware."

In a movie, you know, this would've been the moment when I'd be cut in two by a spray of machinegun bullets or Crashnitz would pull off his mask to reveal a goat's head. Instead I just felt guilty and stupid.

"And now," Crashnitz says in that whiny amused voice of his, "he concocts this remarkable story of baroque duplicity to spread dissension among the ranks. Now, Daniel," he croons, "why on earth would we have any interest in eliminating the very people helping us accomplish our goals here?"

"Well," I says, "let's get things dear, how do you know what Bobby Larkin told me?"

"Because Bobby Larkin told Chip he told you," Mavis says. "Bragging how he'd fucked up the deal here. You know how junkies are. Can't keep their mouths shut." Coming from a junkie, I thought this was pretty bold, but of course Mavis can afford her smack so she doesn't see herself in that light. From the glitter in his eyes you can see Chip isn't just chipping anymore, and Mavis, forget it. Gone.

Stanley spoke for the first time. Stanley has a way of standing in a room real quiet that makes you feel you're on a talk show and he's, like, the host's sidekick. He motioned with his meaty paws like he was wringing the neck of a large chicken: "I'd like to strangle the little fucker, personally."

"As we all would, I'm sure," Crashnitz sighs, wobbling his cane, "if we were the kind of people who went around strangling or otherwise eliminating ingrates and lying junkies, but the facts are obviously otherwise. Kiss the bride and buy yourself a little line or two, Danny boy, and let's talk turkey."

It's two in the afternoon and I haven't slept since yesterday, I'm going to drop this in the mailbox downstairs and write you the rest of it when I've had about ten hours of z's. Things are starting to move very fast now and your mind will start doing nasty shit unless you have dreams to put things together again.

In case something happens to me, if you feel like going to the law you've got all the details. I'm not trying to be melodramatic, for your own good I wouldn't get involved. And maybe this will go by the numbers after all, whatever the numbers are. But what I mainly want to say is, you can laugh, but I love you. I never had the guts or wherewithal to tell you all the times I was fucking you and when you said you couldn't see me anymore I thought maybe you glommed how I felt and that was why you put an end to it. You even stopped answering my letters even though it was your idea. I don't delude myself that the letters mean anything more to you than material for some book, but I wrote them so you would know completely what my life is, for what, for what, maybe I want your pity and maybe I want your pity to magically turn into love, what the fuck do I know about it, or about you, as far as that goes. I worshipped your asshole, man, every time I was inside you the rest of time went away and sometimes I even fucking believed in God. And the way we could talk to each other in bed, right after we came, that dreamy quiet way we'd touch each other and say anything that came into our brains, or nothing at all. I know you think you're not pretty, that's why you've been paying for it all this time, but to me, J., you're movie star beautiful, I mean it. Oh, fuck, forget I said it.

I guess I left off on my wedding night. Crashnitz gave me a little speech about how society doesn't really function anymore according to any workable rules and reality is really about supply and demand. The so-called values of the society are imposed by an elite that doesn't observe them on a mass population that's kept just barely in line by vague notions of right and wrong the ruling class kind of selects bits and pieces of from religion and all the other charismatic elements like patriotism and nationalism, stuff that allows people to identify with a mob, Us against Them, and when you study the behavior of the ruling classes you discover something colder and more machine-like in operation than what happens lower down the food chain, where so-called emotions and these mob impulses come into play. He talked about the Veil of Maya and the indifference of the Cosmos to the feeble efforts of human beings to organize life. Then he shows me the front page of the *New York Times,* the story where the Supreme Court made kidnapping legal when it's the government kidnapping suspected criminals from foreign countries. Now, Lindner, he says, is not a criminal per se, by the lights of so-called society, but let's look at the government for a moment as a sort of gang that services its own needs. Look around you, Crashnitz said. It no longer feeds the hungry, it doesn't house the homeless, it lets the streets and the city fall into ruin. Its only purpose is to keep money in the hands of the people who have always had all the money, and to keep everyone else under control.

So the concept of justice, the equal-under-the-law idea, is really designed to punish the unsuccessful criminal rather than enforce the law across the board. If you're black, for example, you are unsuccessful by definition. So say you commit on a small scale, robbing a drugstore, what the successful white CEO like Lindner does on a vast scale with hostile takeovers and leveraged buyouts or simply looting a financial institution for millions of dollars— and in Lindner's case, with this genetics engineering shit, they're putting stuff in out food that's probably destroying the balance of nature such as it is, maybe causing mutations that will wipe out all life on earth a little further down the line—your black criminal will rot on Riker's Island for five or ten years, while your large-scale white criminal will perhaps pay a fine or get immunity for turning someone else in, and if he does do time it will be in a resort prison not all that different than his Connecticut home. And the global criminals, the ones gouging billions from here there and everywhere, not only never go to jail but in fact run the government from behind the scenes, finance elections, buy senators and congressmen, their companies poison the air everybody has to breathe and the water everybody has to drink, and the only purpose of this gang is to perpetuate itself and its ownership of everything.

We, on the other hand, Crashnitz told me, are doing something with a certain elegant karmic balance. We save a life by taking, admittedly by force, a surplus organ from someone who can live a full and barely interrupted life without it: redistributing the wealth, biologically speaking. These matters are all very relative, and I don't see, he says, where the issue of conscience enters into it at all, unless we revert to infantile and self-defeating forms of hypocrisy.

This wasn't the first time Crashnitz had laid out his philosophy of stealing internal organs and so forth, but it was the first time I heard it with Chip on my lap in a wedding dress with his ass crunching into my boner and six lines of coke up my schnozz, and I have to admit, it was pretty compelling, like that Fritz Lang movie *Dr. Mabuse*, where he lays out how he's going to sabotage the railroads and destroy the economy with a flood of fake currency and so on. Stanley was handing around pieces of wedding cake and we're all munching away getting frosting all over our faces, and the mood, you know, became pretty convivial, Mavis attacked the piano again with some lighthearted favorites like "These Foolish Things," which I remembered was the credit theme of Pasolini's *Salo* but the implications of that didn't really cut through the coke. I mean I didn't flash on the wedding scene where they've all eaten shit and the boy's dressed up as the bride of the skinny libertine and looks like totally miserable with ca-ca all over his face. No, it only crossed my mind later on, after the final details of the snatch were settled and my junkie bride and 1 had spent about four hours of extremely fancy fucking in this

Casa Bella boudoir on the third floor and I'd like crawled out into the dawn, back up to Twenty-Eighth Street. I bought some fruit and cigarettes and several bottles of soda water and the tabloids from the Koreans' on the corner and went upstairs. I played my message tape, which was full.

Hi, Danny, it's Steven on Eighty-Second Street, I'd like to get together with you. Seven eight eight, nine seven eight oh.

Danny, it's Rick, we met a couple weeks ago, maybe you remember. Give me a call. Six seven three four four one two.

Hey Danny, Michael Stein here, that was really some evening last Tuesday. I'm in town all this week, you've got the number.

Just these endless, normal voices.

Note the postmark, Utah, take my word for it this is one state you can skip in this incarnation. I'm in a motel with pinewood panels and pink pleated shades on the lamps and some Mormon literature in the night table. The motel bar has a stuffed eagle with a stuffed rattlesnake hanging out of its beak and I can usually hear somebody breaking a bottle over somebody else's head from my room, folks around here like a little mayhem to perk up their stupid lives, I guess.

I mailed you that postcard from Cleveland just so you wouldn't freak out and do something stupid like call the police. A lot of heavy shit went down at the last minute and needless to say, writing a letter was the last thing on my mind. It's all scrambled up in my head because I've been driving across the country for the past four days. I have this friend in Tucson who teaches at Pima College and says I can stay with him until the heat blows over. Who knows, maybe I'll have my credits from Rutgers transferred to the U of A if they have a decent architecture department, which I doubt. More likely I will head down to Mexico.

Okay, here's what went down. I wake up some time in the afternoon of the big day, totaled from coke, take a shower, my dick's sore from fucking Chip and my ass aches from Chip fucking me, I would like to know how somebody on skag like that keeps a hard-on. I'm brain-dead from the night before with phlegm and crap in my throat, so I drink a quart of OJ, wonder if my absence of physical tension is the symptom of a brain tumor, roll the events of the night before through the mangle of my paranoia, which instead of making me tense is making me like deathly calm and that's somehow much worse, but okay, I fix myself a soothing cup of spearmint tea and concentrate on this guy Lindner and these photos Stanley took with a telephoto lens, like I said he looked a lot like John Cassavetes, not as handsome or distinguished or anything, but human, you know, not like that Exxon guy that disappeared a couple weeks earlier. By now I'm not even considering the so-called moral issues but just like whether I'm in any type of mental or physical shape to pull this off, you know, it's like, what can I eat or pour into myself to get my equilibrium? Fortunately, you bounce back pretty quick at my age, especially if you work out.

The tabloids are full of stories about these hotel fires of mysterious origin, described as "suspicious," like what isn't, plus that rental pussy high school student on Long Island who shot her pimp's wife. The front page of the *Post* says PIMP OR LOVER?, like they don't have enough imagination to put PIMP *AND* LOVER, the usual configuration actually, and there's another moral crusade going on, that Quayle doofus is in town shitting his millionaire diapers about the "cultural elite," it says he went to a spelling bee in New Jersey and this twelve-year-old wrote "potato" on the blackboard and Quayle like corrected him by putting an "e" on the end, I like that, it's appropriate if you look around, this "cultural elite" shit is just a code word for fags and Jews, frankly I don't know one Jew or one homosexual who can't spell "potato" correctly, I would guess even the skankiest rent boys I've run across could manage "potato," I dunno, maybe not, but they wouldn't be proud about it if they couldn't, this kind of shit makes me sad, what can I say, that somebody who can't even spell "potato" is like one of those people pulling the strings that Crashnitz was talking about. It was all beginning to make sense and that made me sad, too.

So I turn the page, hoping to find Cindy Adams sucking up to the usual wives of military dictators and delivering her tart observations, I think tart is exactly the right word, from beyond the grave of six dozen facelifts, and I find this story about Stagpole, whose like decline has somewhat faded out of the news for a few months. Well, more tragedy, him and his strumpet are not only splitsville but she's written a Sandy Miller–type novel about him, even though "revelations" about their marriage are like prohibited by their divorce settlement. Boo hoo. But then I read further down the column and there's some stuff about his kids, the ones that were like fathered by the bell captain at the Stagpole Palace, one's in school in Switzerland, another one's vacationing in Carriacou, and the third—

I'm no master of suspense, J., I read the item twice and then dropped my cigarette. As you maybe know, Tina Stagpole was what they call "ailing" and in serious shape from an obscure liver disease that the doctors now felt could only be treated by transplant surgery.

I think: it's a mistake, maybe there's something about it in the *News*, which is generally more accurate anyway, so I flip through that and sure enough there's another story, slightly different angle, the strumpet's been spending a lot of time seeking spiritual advice from Cardinal O'Connor, aka Katrina according to Bobby Larkin, who really ought to know, supposedly about strumpet's divorce as a Catholic and all, and kind of parenthetically they mention Tina Stagpole's "grave" medical condition, and what can I tell you, we don't put "liver" on the menu at the Emerson Club when we're serving kidney, and I don't figure two of the tabloids would get the same detail wrong, either. So, I mean, unless Lindner was some extraordinary freak of nature with a matching set, removing the item in question would put us into murder one rather than Robin Hood territory. Which also, obviously, gave the Bobby Larkin scenario a brand-new credibility.

This is all for now. It's creeping me out just putting this on paper. I'll send you the rest when I get out of Utah.

Okay, where was I . . . it doesn't matter.

Mavis had transformed herself all over again, back to the ratty blond hair and so forth, but with some

brand-new touches, for example a dozen clanking brace-
lets on each arm, and a green mylar dress that made
her breasts look strange, fishnet black stockings and
red heels and a makeup job which, given her square
chin and all, gave the very faint impression of like an
incipient beard, also, she'd put something in her hair
that made it look, I don't know, drag queeny, it was all
very subtle but you just knew anybody who didn't know
her would think twice what her gender was. Now that I
think about it, for all I know Mavis might've been a boy
in a former life, I mean I've fucked a few transsexuals
and if the indoor plumbing is like properly installed
it's really hard to tell the difference. As far as that goes,
most women will tell you how guys go craziest fucking
them in the ass, their fixation for pussy or whatever
notwithstanding. I think sex is all in the head anyway.
What's that word, chimerical.

She sat in the back of the car, a big black Cadillac four-
door, polishing this tight sinuous smile with a stick of pink
lip gloss, her eyes starry not from dope but anticipation.
Stanley behind the wheel wearing light blue chauffeur's
livery, looking more than ever like Eddie Constantine in
Alphaville, like a heavily armed, hundred-year-old crus-
tacean, and Chip on the passenger side in front, with his
goofy Chip look, that "every day's a new day and every day
I'm wasted" effect, in a dirty flannel shirt and ripped jeans,
the Port of Authority look. I'd put on a black T-shirt and
navy pants, plus I was wearing a khaki raincoat with big
pockets. Warm night.

"Hi, hon," Mavis says all cheery, like we're driving
down to the Village to catch some jazz.

"Nine oh five," Stanley announces, checking his watch.

"I figure," Chip pipes up, "we hang out at the Ramada or one of the theater bars until eleven."

We had already gone over everything a million times. Chip and I would go into La Esqualita separately ahead of Mavis and kind of melt in with the crowd, keeping an eye on Lindner. It seems he went there every Thursday night without fail, standing or sitting through a drag show and if he scored he'd leave with his date after that, if he didn't score he'd stay there until three or so then head up to Sally II. We figured Mavis to be more his type than myself or Chip in drag, like I told you before, we're both too mannish, but if he didn't go for the bait we were ready to grab him out on the street, unless of course he scored, in which case we'd follow him plus date to whatever hotel and wait for his trisexual encounter to hit the road. According to Stanley the date always left before Lindner did, the only trouble being that Lindner sometimes fucked with them for two hours instead of one, if he scored early in the night that wouldn't be much of a problem, but say he grabbed something in Sally's after threeish, and fucked for two hours, the dawn would be coming up in the street and we'd have to kind of use our judgment whether to take him then or another time. Our best bet was Mavis. Otherwise the variables multiplied. He might hit La Esqualita three times in a week, even more than that, but you couldn't depend on it, and of course if we had to start showing up there every night looking for him we'd undoubtedly draw attention, witnesses would remember us and so forth.

Ideally, we'd nab him a couple dozen yards from La Esqualita because it's a real dark street where people kind of expect shit to occur, so you don't get any loitering types or casual foot traffic in the dead of night. But okay, in case it got complicated we had certain assets: Stanley for one, second this rag soaked in chloroform Chip carried in a baggie in one of his pockets. If the mark tricked with Mavis, see, we were going to approach them like a pair of muggers. I had a gun Crashnitz gave me in the pocket of my raincoat, I had no idea if it was loaded or what the fuck, I never fired a gun in my life or even held one until then, unless you count my father's shotgun. And that I only, like, fondled. Guns scare the crap out of me. Guy's got a knife, you might have a chance, but a gun, man, one bang and that's the ballgame.

I can tell you what the cocktail lounge at the Ramada's like, think of dark Formica and grainy indirect lighting and emotions collecting in front of you in the little puddles formed by your cocktail glass, islands and continents of feelings you don't know how to place any more, and voices, the so-called human element, that remind you you're chained to the earth by a million little details: the world has fancy intellectual names for all these manacles and torture devices holding you down, but they might as well be called Mavis and Stanley and Chip, or the boy who ran away from home to learn fear, or the boy you love beyond anything who brings you a souvenir from his trip to Easter Island with the one he wants to fuck instead of you, or just a client whose loneliness and despair jut out on his face in the seconds before he comes: to me they were faces scribbled in watercolor drooling down the window, drizzling into Eighth Avenue and puddling up with all the human wreckage stashed in waterlogged corners of construction scaffolds.

So, maybe I found my will in the Ramada Inn, who knows, in a glass of champagne, while Mavis was telling Stanley: "It's just that you *look* so heavy, sweetheart, that's got nothing to do with your . . . how can I say it, *heart.*"

"Fuck, Mavis, you know I've got a major heart."

"Mmm-hmm, big as all outdoors. Maybe we can use it some time."

"Shit," Chip cackles, "you're an old fucking crocodile, Stanley."

"You're implying I'm what, a reptile?"

"Get over it, you're one of the good kind. The, uh, professional type."

"I've been professional," Mavis chuckles, beaming her eye shadow into an icy expanse of Jack Daniels, "and I've been amateur."

"An inspired amateur," Stanley wheezes, shaking his head, "will show you shit a pro never fucking figured out."

"And amateur is more fun," Mavis says, but nobody's listening so she looks out the window.

"That's what I'm saying," Chip brays. "One you can learn from. Young guys, fucking setting out in the world, they got no role models. So they follow the goddamn fashions, see what I mean."

Stanley coughed into his cocktail napkin and dabbled his lips in a dainty kind of way. Then he looked real serious: "Kid," he says to Chip, pushing his uniformed forearm halfway across the table and sticking his thumb out like a blackboard pointer, "the one thing you're gonna learn from me, and I'll tell you nothin' else—"

'You're such an asshole, Stanley," Mavis tells him. "The only thing he *might* learn from you is how to hit a pothole at forty miles an hour when he sees it coming two blocks away. That's what I love about you . . ."

"Nothin' else, baby," Stanley says, totally ignoring her, and now his eyes are like boring holes into Chip, whose teeth are all pink from the neon in the window. And he lurches forward a little more and fixes Chip with that pre-historic face that's launched a thousand really bum trips in places like the men's room at Bloomingdale's.

A moment of silence. Mavis is anxious to start talking and stares at her Jack Daniels. Then, with a certain fuck-it-all bravado, she lifts the glass to her mouth and swallows it all down, holds it in front of her eyes like a zircon choker she's appraising.

"Beware of pity." Stanley rasps it out like it's the last thing the old turtle is ever gonna say. But Mavis breaks in real quick: "I second that emotion." She thwacks the glass down on her napkin and zaps Stanley with her movie star smile and a little shake to her bosoms. "Even if you are an asshole."

Chip like arches back in his seat and plants his forearms down on the table, like, "now the Quaker meeting has begun, Amen," and says: "After we dump him—"

"SHUT THE FUCK UP," Mavis screams, still smiling her Queen of the Moon smile, and grabs his pants under the table and squeezes. "We don't talk DUMP, we don't talk HIM, look at me when I talk to you, sweetheart, you get one more of those"—meaning his Heineken—"and listen, who am I? Who's this here?"

Chip looks at her as if it's his mother, then he examines his fingernails.

"We're not gonna fight," he says, half-hopeful. "Hey," Stanley says. He moves his chin about a quarter of an inch, like totally the father of us all. "We're gonna have another very light cocktail, we're gonna breathe in and out the way we all do, and then, kids . . . we're gonna do our jobs, nice and even and everybody as a team."

Mavis looks at me with that cracked expression she gets when things get too reality-oriented.

"Danny," she winks, "I think my tits look too real." Well, you get the idea. La Esqualita had some serious Attica alumni checking IDs and collecting the tariff in this dim noir downstairs vestibule, but they waved me in, Chip had gone in first and like vanished in this swirl of sleazy enchantment where mirror-ball effects like rolled across two hundred faces and challenging wardrobe selections, wigs and earrings, for some reason reality never quite coincides with what you imagine. In my brain I'd slowed the place down to a tea dance and there was like this outrageous house stuff blasting from every part of the place and queens on the dance floor flouncing and parading very regal, Versailles at seventy-eight rpm if you remember records, tons of bystanders crowding up to the tables which were like fully occupied by jumped-up persons of color from the *New York Times* and their slickered dates, the kind that wear like perfect vermillion lip gloss and gardenias in their waved hair, remaindered couture dresses from Century 21, this type of thing, plus off-duty him and her chippies from like the Port of Authority in the clothes they change into to become hip and happening instead of on duty, personality blazing across their mugs like a facial peel, of course I can't see Chip anywhere, there's a sea of motion and I've got one eye on the door expecting Mavis and also I don't see Lindner anywhere, it's this chaos, and

I thought, fuck it, let's just, you know, party, so I stroll over to the bar and buy myself a Rémy Martin, with a soda back, and when it comes I take a sip of soda with this oozing sensation that life is very precious, even right now. I feel the weight of the gun in my pocket and think, what wiggy shit we get ourselves into, but it all passes. It really does.

Mavis stepped into the whirling orange light from the disco ball and looked around, real disoriented, then made for the central dance floor area and the tables with this determined look. I lost sight of her in the crowd, and next thing I know Chip's standing beside me kind of hopping around like he's dancing.

"I don't see that guy in here," he says.

Now it's Madonna's "Vogue" from the DJ booth, a little out of date but you just know twenty queens from San Juan hit the stage at that point voguing themselves into a frenzy. I like nodded at Chip to follow me into the packed darker regions of the club, along the side of the dance floor. Just past the side tables there's this smaller raised platform with, on one side, the dressing room where all the scheduled drag queens are fooling with their hair and making out with their boyfriends, there's an open doorway and also a big window cut in the side of the dressing room, inside past the room itself there's some sort of corridor, so you can follow this drama of half-dressed transvestites and their heavy dates moving back and forth, and then on the other side at the end there's a toilet. There's like ten or so people flailing around on this smaller riser. I lead Chip through the dancers, here there's these rows of pink lights that flash on and then fade out leaving a kind of deep twilight residue and then darkness.

I pull him into the little bathroom. He's, like, glazed.

"Look, give me that shit in your pants, okay? And you take the gun."

"Fuck, Danny, what the fuck?"

"It's just easier," I said, meaning nothing. Chip's sitting on the toilet seat and digging a strip of aluminum foil from his pocket. He unfolds it and there's a little patch of heroin powder in there. He brings it to his nose and sniffs, holds it out: "How 'bout a taste, Uncle Dan?"

I looked away from him.

"Hey, we're married now, right?"

I grabbed him and pulled him off the toilet. I caught the edge of the baggie and yanked it out of his pocket.

"Look," I say, dropping him to his knees, and I show him the gun, kind of wave it in his face. "You ever give this thing your full attention, Chip? Or are you just too fucked to live?"

He like stares at the gun and then his hand comes up dreamlike and closes around my wrist real tight. He closes his eyes.

"Oh man," he says, "I thought about everything a million times, a million times."

And he opens his mouth wide and jerks my arm and pulls the gun barrel into his mouth like it's somebody's cock. The fingers of my other hand were like fumbling with the zip-lock on the baggie and outside somebody's knocking on the toilet door, shit, Chip's still got his eyes closed and now he's sucking the gun, real loud, drool pouring out the sides of his mouth. I had to steady the baggie against my gun hand and finally pulled out the rag and stuffed it under his nose, I'm squatted down and he drops the rest of the way to the floor, on his face.

I put the rag back into the baggie and stuffed it into my raincoat with the gun, then pulled the door open.

"Some asshole's passed out in here," I tell the guy standing there, and move past him real fast, back through the maze of bodies to this wide corridor in back that's full of little groups of people. I'm scanning the whole time for Mavis, that green mylar, but now they've got a strobe light on and I just see flashes and streaks of glitter and fabrics and hair and pieces of faces, stumbling through the blackness at the back toward the bar where the lighting's normal. And guess what, Lindner was there, practically where he stood the first time I saw him, alone.

I didn't waste any time. I walked right up to him and he saw me coming and for a second he smiled like you would at anybody and I said: "Mr. Lindner, don't ask any questions, you wanna stay out of deep shit tonight you come with me now. Outta here."

He starts to say something but first of all I knew his name and he must've got some type of telepathic wave that this was like for real, because he nodded with this scared look. Then I gave him a little peek at the gun, that was enough for him. He headed for the entrance with me right behind him. I started walking beside him up the stairs and said: "When we get out of here turn left and start walking as fast as you can but make it look normal. There's a car parked about twenty yards up the street to the right with a guy in it who's looking out for you. When we get to Ninth Avenue we're gonna turn left and flag the first cab we see."

"Look," he says, "what exactly—"

"I'm gonna explain but I can't do it now. Let's keep moving."

One advantage, just as we're coming out a whole horde of Mardi Gras types is pouring out of taxis, the street's blocked and even though the headlights are making the sidewalk a real proscenium I figure Stanley's view was hazed by all the queens shrieking and clambering out of the taxis. Lindner did exactly as I told him and once we made the corner, which was like eternity as they say because they're long blocks in that neighborhood, I knew we'd, you know, eluded the A-team for the moment. So we got one of the cabs headed downtown from Esqualita.

"Be real normal," I told him getting in.

I took him to an all-night coffee shop on the Lower East Side. He looked freaked, like he'd been beamed into somebody else's bad acid trip, but once he understood I wasn't going to off him or what have you he just listened while I ran it down for him. Once in a while he'd say some thing, like, "That's incredible," or "I just can't believe I'm hearing this." I could see he didn't exactly believe my story, either, he was still trying to figure out how I knew his name. He kept ordering cup after cup of decaf and pouring half and half into it. First I told him the general outline, you know, without using any names, but since he seemed skeptical I finally gave him the rest of it.

In the bright light Lindner didn't look half bad. He had that athletic middle-aged look that goes with tennis whites. His face was what you'd call benevolent, I guess, a good listener. His hands shook holding the coffee cup but he was calming down bit by bit. It was only one in the morning, really. By the time I finished the story Lindner had relaxed on his side of the booth and got this like philosophical look in his eyes, which were this really piercing dark blue color I've only seen on one other person, a playwright who drops into the Emerson Club from time to time and quietly drinks an entire bottle of Stoli all by himself in a banquette and then leaves a hundred-dollar tip under his unused napkin.

He had extremely slender wrists that poked from the cuffs of his pinstriped shirt. I thought of how difficult it is to buy jewelry for wrists that thin.

"You've done a pretty noble thing," he said. "I mean my God, you've saved my life."

"Yeah, well, I just figured it was wrong, Mr. Lindner. By my own code of things anyways."

"The question is," he said, "what can I do for you? How much did these people offer you for the kidnapping?"

"Oh, man, forget it, I don't want anything. I wanna like take my savings and split town before they like come after me or something."

Lindner winked.

"Oh, now, Danny, I think you'd like *something* for your trouble, wouldn't you?"

I thought about that. Well, fuck, I like money. "Hey," I said, "if you could see your way clear to giving me some little reward—"

And suddenly Lindner was sliding out of the booth and standing up looking down at me.

"Frankly," he said, "this is a pretty elaborate scam, Danny, and if I were you I'd hit on people who dig what you've got to offer and leave the others alone. I don't imagine you're stupid enough to shoot me in here. You're lucky I'm not screaming bloody murder. I thought this was some very original come-on, but it's obvious that you're crazy.

You're cute, baby, if you had a set of tits I'd fuck you hard, but no way do I believe this insane story of yours. What kind of name is Crashnitz supposed to be, anyway? You sound like you're all coked up, is that it?" He was digging out his wallet. "People like you have to watch that stuff, kid. It does bad things to your brain." He threw a fifty dollar bill on the table and walked out of the coffee shop oozing enough disgust for the five or six skanky patrons at the counter to notice it.

I left some bills for the coffee and ran out of the place just in time to see Stanley sap the guy upside the head and toss him into the back of the Cadillac.

Well, J., that's about all she wrote, except for the last part, which is also the worst part and the main reason I'm now in Guadalajara. At least it's not humid, but I've had the shits for three days running and it's hard for me even to hold a pen, I'm that wasted from dysentery.

Maybe it all happened the way I told you and maybe none of it happened at all, how do you like that? Let's say the guy did get interested in Mavis and Chip and I followed them into the street and pulled the hold-up scenario, Mavis like feigning hysteria while Chip knocked Lindner out with the chloroform. And then we drove him over to the clinic, laid him out in the operating room, extracted his usable parts, and then dumped his body in the Rambles the following night, which is where it was actually found, minus plenty of goodies Crashnitz could peddle for a sultan's ransom. And instead of getting wasted, Chip and me both got paid a bonus for our loyalty and good service to the company.

That would be a type of happy ending for yours truly, honeymooning in Mexico with the prettiest dick the Port of Authority has ever known, unfortunately happy endings have not been my thing in what passes for real life. Tell you what I did, I went up to the baths in Harlem. If you've never been to the baths in Harlem, J., I advise you to keep it that way. Once when I told you something that sounded like stupidly cocky and self-assured you said, Well, wait till you've had a few decades of disappointment and see how you feel about it then. It's the last thing I thought of before I passed out in one of the cubicles, which have roaches and shit and smell like bad feet and ammonia mixed with resin from crack pipes. If you've never had sex in the baths in Harlem with a guy you're not only not attracted to but find repulsive in every respect, had sex with that guy not because you want sex but because you want to finally prove to yourself that you don't exist, you don't know what disappointment is.

And when I woke up I had no idea where I was, it took several minutes to figure it out, then I remembered I had this half-formed plan in my brain, get the car out of Twenty-Sixth Street, bring it around to the apartment, pack as much shit as I could carry off and then goodbye. Even if the ghouls of Gramercy Park decided to leave me alone, this like pall of doom had settled over everything.

It was late in the morning. I got to the parking lot right when workers from the insurance company next door started coming out for lunch. There were clouds in the sky, gray clouds. Even behind the wheel of my car I felt trapped in some awful movie like that black-and-white Japanese film about making pornography that's full of these shots of huge carp in fish tanks that just goes on and on, I felt like one of those pornographic carp.

I parked on Twenty-Eighth Street almost in front of my building. I went up in the elevator and then down the hall to my door. I had my key out, I went to put it in the lock, then saw the door was a little open, not open exactly but off the lock. So my heart begins pounding and I think, Oh shit, they're gonna do me. At the same moment I pushed the door all the way open, thinking, I don't know, I'd like startle them and then run down the stairs or something.

It's a floor-through, the door opens into the middle of the main space, facing a long green wall with three windows set along it. Then I've got the bedroom, the kitchen, the bathroom partitioned off. The first thing I see is HA HA HA splashed across the wall in real jumpy-looking red letters, like they were swabbed on there with a mop. The next thing I see is the bridal veil from Chip's wedding outfit lying on the floor, I didn't recognize it right away, but there was wind coming in the front windows that ruffled it, and then I saw Chip, after I stepped into the room, because he was propped up against the wall beside the door, he was naked, and something had torn him open from his neck to his belly and pulled his ribs apart so the middle of him looked like a carcass in a slaughterhouse. And his . . . genitals had been sliced off and stuffed in the cavity so the head of his dick stuck out of this rip in his lower abdomen.

When I finished vomiting I sat for a long time looking out the window with nothing in my brain except HA HA HA, and of course to them it probably had been a good joke. There was blood everywhere but I guess they did him in the bathtub because most of it was in there.

So many strange things went through my head, J. I thought of the first time I met Chip and the first time I made it with Chip and how I'd felt about him years ago, like everything he said or did was important and precious, even stuff that was fucked up, and all the time I spent figuring him out, getting like his background, his life story, watching the way he operated in the bars and the bus station, I mean I was three times more educated than he was but for a long time there I followed him around like a dog, grateful if he noticed me, etcetera etcetera. Of course we went through a lot of changes with that and in the end I felt sorry for him more than I loved him. But you know, you look at the body of someone you loved all torn apart that way, and it's maybe even worse if they'd become, like, an object of pity before reaching that state. They gutted him, basically, and took out whatever they could use. So he really looked like a pile of garbage with a pretty face.

I sat in the same spot for twelve hours. After about six hours I knew what I would have to do, and then I spent another six thinking out how to do it, and then I got into bed, I slept I don't know how long, and then I moved the body back into the bathtub and. turned the shower on. I got a mop and sponges and bleach and Comet and all this cleaning shit from under the sink and started working on the walls, the floors, every place there was blood. The hardest to get rid of was the HA HA HA, that took almost an hour of scrubbing.

I went out and walked over to Lexington Avenue and bought a butcher's knife and a hacksaw, and a box of Hefty garbage bags with the tie-up pull-tops. I went home. All afternoon and evening the messages kept coming in, from all the scat queens and foot fetishists and aging bum boys desperate to like worship at the temple, while I chopped and sawed Chip into pieces that would go in a garbage bag without the bones sticking through the plastic. It's hard work. I didn't put too much of him in any one bag.

Then I took him down to the car, in three trips, using a pink plastic laundry basket to pile the bags in. I went back up and scrubbed the bathtub and looked around for bloodstains, then I drove down to the East Village and left one bag in front of Kevin's house, and another one in a trashcan where one of Chip's regular tricks lives. I crossed to the West Village on Ninth Street and stopped at several addresses where Chip and I had done customers together, leaving a bag at each address. I put three in Chelsea, and then I carried a real small one into the Port Authority and pushed it into a trash container. Then it was finished.

I kept his prick for a souvenir.

The next day they arrested some people in connection with the missing Exxon executive, and I gave my notice to the landlord. I sold most of my stuff at the flea market that Saturday. I didn't answer any calls. On Sunday, I packed the car and left. Incidentally, J., Danny isn't my real name, either. I don't have a real name. I live where nothing has a name, and the rest is silence.

McNally Editions reissues books that are not widely known but have stood the test of time, that remain as singular and engaging as when they were written. Available in the US wherever books are sold or by subscription from mcnallyeditions.com.